NANCY WARREN

A TONI DIAMOND MYSTERY

ISBN: ebook 978-1-928145-09-7

ISBN: print 978-1-928145-10-3

Cover Design by Stunning Book Covers

Ambleside Publishing

INTRODUCTION

Toni Diamond wins a cruise. Will the real prize be murder?

Toni Diamond, makeup artist to middle America, boards a cruise ship planning to enjoy seven days of sun, sea and relaxation. She's taking her rebellious almost-seventeen year old daughter Tiffany and her Dolly Parton-crazed mother, Linda, along for the treat. Unfortunately, the cruise isn't all bliss. Between mysterious disappearances, an outbreak of Norovirus and her sense of impending doom, Toni's barely got a moment to relax in one of the striped lounge chairs. But is there really something sinister going on or is Toni imagining things?

PRAISE FOR THE TONI DIAMOND MYSTERIES

FROSTED SHADOW

"This series is first class. Super intrigue and great characters."

— LINDA

ULTIMATE CONCEALER

"Never a dull moment. Nancy Warren is a true entertainer."

— BELINDA WILSON

MIDNIGHT SHIMMER

"Fantastic from start to finish."

— PATTI SANDERS

A DIAMOND CHOKER FOR CHRISTMAS

"I loved every minute of the book."

— GAIL A. DEMAREE

MIDNIGHT SHIMMER

CHAPTER 1

They say travel broadens the mind; but you must have the mind.

— G.K. CHESTERTON

At my age, travel broadens the behind.

— STEPHEN FRY

*T*oni Diamond zipped up her lilac-colored travel case and wheeled it to the front door. For about the tenth time she confirmed that she had her passport, the boarding passes for the cruise ship, and the boarding passes for the flight that she'd printed from her home computer.

Since she was a few minutes early, she checked her appearance in the hall mirror, then dug out her mini makeup bag and freshened her lipstick.

"I hope I brought enough shoes," her mother said, dragging the largest suitcase on wheels that Toni had ever seen.

"Mama, we're only going to be on the cruise for seven

days. How many pairs of shoes do you think you're going to need?"

"You'd be surprised," Linda Plotnik said. "Between the formal dinners and lunches and the cocktail parties and the shore excursions, a girl can never have too many pairs of shoes."

Toni was never one to argue with the obvious. Instead, she raised her voice. "Tiffany? Honey? Are you ready?"

Sounds that could have been mistaken for the wail of the newly raised dead reached her ears, faint but plaintive.

"Yep, I guess she's ready."

"He'd better be on time," Linda said, peering out the front window.

"Luke is always on time," Toni said, and barely had she finished speaking when Luke Marciano pulled into her drive. His tough-guy cop's eyes were hidden behind dark shades. He was driving the latest of the vintage cars and trucks that he bought and fixed up in his spare time. This one was a navy-blue Chevrolet Nova, 1968, and she only knew this because it had been all he could talk about the last few weeks. She supposed it was better than hearing about his day job, which, since he was a Dallas detective, could be pretty gory at times.

"Tiffany? Luke's here," she yelled upstairs.

Her daughter, who would turn seventeen aboard the *Duchess of the Caribbean* in less than a week, walked toward them with all the youthful vigor of a ninety-year-old breathing her last. "I can't believe you're making me do this."

"One day, honey, you can write about me in your memoirs —about how cruel I was, forcing you to go on a Caribbean cruise—but for now, we need to get going."

Tiffany's only answer was a dramatic eye roll. At least her daughter had abandoned the Goth look. Toni was naturally biased, but she thought Tiffany was on her way to being a beauty, with long dark hair, blue eyes, and the most engaging smile—when she bothered to smile. Dwayne Diamond, her father, had been useless for most things, but the man had passed on some fine DNA in the looks department. Fortunately, Tiffany had not inherited his intelligence or his morals.

Toni opened the door before Luke reached it. He walked in, giving her a quick kiss. "You girls all ready?"

"Please don't make me go," Tiff appealed to the cop.

He looked as sympathetic as Toni had ever seen him. "I feel for you, believe me, I do, but somebody's got to look after your mom."

Toni turned on him. "Are you saying I can't look after myself?" Really, after bringing up a daughter singlehandedly and building a successful business in the cosmetics industry, she found his chauvinism a little hard to handle.

He pulled off his sunglasses and leveled his steely cop stare at her. "The last time I let you out of my sight, you got shot."

It wasn't as though she'd *intended* to be attacked by a crazed killer. She stuck her nose in the air, and it was a large nose, so the gesture meant something. "I doubt anyone will try to shoot me on board a cruise ship."

"And that's the only reason I'm driving you to the airport." He came closer, took hold of her shoulders. "But you keep your nose out of places where it doesn't belong," he said. "You hear me?"

"Of course I do."

"Okay, then. Let's go." He turned to grab the bags and nearly stumbled when he saw her suitcase. "Are you kidding me?" he asked.

"What?"

He stared at her bag. The lilac hard-sided case was decorated in fake diamonds that spelled her website address, www.ToniDiamond.com. "You buy that at luggage-is-us?"

"Of course not. I had the case custom made," she said, not without pride. "My name is my brand and every time someone sees my name, I want them to click on my website, where they will discover the wide range of beauty products available from Lady Bianca Cosmetics."

He gazed from her case to Linda's, which made up in sheer size for not having a diamond-encrusted Web address. Also, the bag was bright purple.

Last, he turned to Tiffany's case. It was half the size of her mother's and black. Following Luke's gaze, Toni said, "Honey, you should make your suitcase stand out in some way. Ninety percent of the bags on the carousel at the airport will be black."

"I can recognize mine," Tiffany said. "It's scuffed at the corner. See?" And she pointed to the slight discoloration on one edge of her bag.

"Okay, then," Luke said, ending an argument before it began. He hefted Toni's bag in one hand, hauled Linda's behind him on its wheels, and the three women followed him, Linda and Toni rolling their on board luggage, Tiffany dragging her single-wheeled bag behind her. Her school backpack, slung over her shoulders, contained her computer.

When they got in the car, Linda pulled out a blister pack

of pills and punched one out. She retrieved a bottle of water from her carry-on bag and glugged down a pill.

"What's that, Grandma?" Tiffany asked.

"My airsick pills."

"You get airsick?"

Linda smiled at her. "Not if I take my pills."

She swallowed a second pill. They drove for a couple of miles, then Linda asked, "How many passengers did you say are on this ship?"

"Around three thousand."

Linda jerked upright. "I don't think I brought enough sample packs."

Luke stared at Toni, settled beside him on the bench seat of the old car. "I thought this cruise was supposed to be a holiday?"

"Honey, I won the cruise for having the best sales in the country. You don't seriously think two top saleswomen are going to sit on their butts suntanning while thousands of potential customers surround them every hour of every day?"

Instead of answering her, Luke glanced in the rearview mirror and his gaze connected with Tiffany's. His eyes crinkled in an almost smile. "You know how to swim, kid?"

THEY BADE Luke goodbye at the Dallas airport and waited for their flight. Linda, always a nervous flier, popped another couple of her pills. Two hours later, they arrived safely in Fort Lauderdale, ready to embark on their ship, the *Duchess of the Caribbean*. Toni had never been on a cruise before and she was wildly excited.

The prize had been two tickets and, knowing she couldn't pick her daughter or her mother without somebody's feelings getting hurt (whatever Tiffany said to the contrary), she'd paid extra to bring both of them.

They took a taxi to the terminal and drove what seemed like miles to get to their ship. When the cab let them off, an efficient team took charge of their luggage and directed them to the boarding area.

The ship was moored directly ahead of them and it was enormous, rising like a great skyscraper from the ocean. Linda took one look at the ship, pulled out her packet of pills, and punched another one out of the blister pack.

"I thought those were airsick pills," Tiffany said.

"They also work as seasick pills. I think they're good for any motion sickness." She paused to think. "Well, maybe not rollercoaster sickness. You know, a pill can only do so much."

"Do you get seasick?"

"How should I know? I've never been on a cruise before, but my motto is better safe than sorry."

There was a line to get on board. It was a long line, but Toni enjoyed every minute of it, chatting to the women near her, gazing up and down and mentally cataloging every weakness she and Lady Bianca could fix, from dry skin to outdated eye shadow colors. Once they were close enough to glimpse inside the terminal, they saw ropes cordoning the mass of passengers into another long, snaking line.

"This reminds me of auction day at the stockyards," Linda said, glancing around. "And there are some fattened porkers here that'd bring a pretty price."

"Inside voice, Mama." It was true, though, that pound for pound, cruisers seemed to be a heavier demographic.

"Oh, barf," Tiffany said. Toni followed her gaze to a boisterous group of twenty-somethings piling out of two cabs. The women all wore tight white shorts that barely covered their butts and skipper's caps, as well as identical bright pink T-shirts that said, *Last Stop Before Married*.

"Which one do you think is the bride?"

Tiffany glanced at her. "I'm guessing it's the mean-looking one with the wedding veil underneath her skipper's cap."

"What fun! I bet they're getting married on board."

"You know what's sad? They paid money to get T-shirts printed and the best they could come up with was *Last Stop Before Married*?"

"Not everyone's as smart as you, honey."

"The guys are worse. Check them out."

A matching half dozen young men wore white Bermuda shorts and black T-shirts that said, *Groom Support*. And a beefy guy in the middle had a white shirt that said, *Groom*.

"Well, what they lack in literary talent, they make up in enthusiasm." Or possibly alcohol consumption.

"Are they seriously getting married on board?"

"I guess so. There's a wedding chapel."

"That is so pathetic."

Then the woman in the veil shrieked. "No! Don't let them touch it. Matt? You have to carry the dress."

And the beefy guy obligingly lifted a heavy-looking vinyl garment bag from the arms of one of the porters. The bag was printed with gold lettering from a bridal boutique. "Is she going to make him carry the wedding dress through this whole line? I bet it weighs a ton," Linda said.

"Those shirts should read, *Doom Support*."

Even as she giggled, Toni said, "I think it would be

romantic to get married at sea. Do you think the captain performs the ceremony? In his uniform? I hope he has a British accent. I bet he does."

"If she's already treating him like crap, why is he marrying her?" Tiffany was clearly more interested in the wedding couple than in the mechanics of cruise ship weddings.

"It's probably stress. Brings out the worst in people."

"Maybe they're getting married at sea so he can drop-kick her overboard after the knot is tied and collect the life insurance."

"Tiff! That is an awful thing to say."

"Made you laugh, though," her daughter said with a *gotcha!* grin.

Checking out their fellow passengers helped pass the time and even if Tiffany's comments were mostly sarcastic, at least she was enjoying herself. And making her mother and grandmother laugh.

There were cheerful attendants at various stages along the line, and soon they were herded to a woman who passed them all a health questionnaire. They were asked whether they felt sick, were running a fever, had been ill recently. Had they been exposed to Ebola?

"Reading these questions is making me feel queasy," Linda said.

"Just tick No to everything, Grandma."

"People come on cruise ships with Ebola?"

"I'm sure they don't do it on purpose, Mama."

After about an hour of various lines for different security and boarding procedures, they headed up the gangplank.

Once on board, they were directed to their suite. Naturally, Tiffany had argued that she needed her own stateroom.

Naturally, Toni had disagreed. Instead, she'd booked them all into a suite that consisted of two single beds and a seating area with a pull-out couch.

The room was larger than she'd imagined it would be and resembled a hotel room more than her vaguely romantic notion of bunk beds and portholes. There was a bathroom, a TV, and hotel-room art on the walls, but the showstopper was the double doors out onto the balcony, where the sparkling blue water beckoned. She could see five other cruise ships docked and a spit of land sprouting houses and apartment buildings.

Even Tiffany began to look cheerful. "Let's go up on deck and see what's going on," she suggested. They didn't have their luggage yet, so there wasn't much to do but go out as they were.

They walked a couple of flights up to the Lido deck and found some of their cruising companions had already donned swimwear and were lounging in the pool and hot tubs, or reclining on the deck chairs that were lined up, row upon row. Between the sparkle of sun off waves and sun off suntan oil, she was glad she was wearing her dark glasses.

A live band played rock and roll in one corner and four young people in white shirts and Bermuda shorts led a group of happy looking passengers in the twist.

She contemplated joining them but thought she'd get oriented first.

"Oh, I see the buffet is open," she said, as a man walked by with a tray loaded with a hamburger, a plate heaped with french fries, a slab of lasagna, a pile of taco chips snow-capped with sour cream and dripping with salsa and guacamole, a quarter of a pizza, and a watermelon slice.

"So's the bar," Linda said, heading for the curving outdoor bar. A cheerful guy was serving drinks to half a dozen passengers sitting on stools. "Well, isn't this nice?" she said, bellying up to the bar.

The bartender gave her a huge smile. He seemed like he really loved his work. "What'll you have, pretty lady?"

Linda twinkled at him. "I'll have a martini."

"Mama, you never drink martinis."

"I know, but to prepare for the cruise, I watched *An Affair to Remember* with Deborah Kerr and Cary Grant." She sighed heavily. "And when they were on board they drank cocktails. It looked so sophisticated, I was determined to have a martini as soon as I got aboard." She pulled out her cruise card, which was connected to her credit card. "Drinks are on me, girls. What'll y'all have?"

"Tiffany?"

Her daughter was in that miserable stage where she was too young to drink and too old to get excited about a Shirley Temple. "I'll have sparkling water, please."

"Toni?"

The bartender's brass nametag said his name was Romeo and he came from the Philippines. "What do you suggest, Romeo?"

"You like rum? You like fruit?"

She nodded.

"You leave it to me."

He was more fun to watch than the band or the twisting dancers as he boogied his way to the ice, made a performance out of adding the rum and juices and the bright red straw, then danced the drink over to her without missing a beat or spilling a drop.

She laughed. "Thank you, sir."

The three women raised glasses and sipped.

Toni loved people-watching. She loved the quirks and oddities, the beautiful people and the ones who maybe spent too much of their cruise time at the buffet and ought to get out more. There were extremely old people walking with the aid of canes or walkers and young couples wearing wedding rings so self-consciously shiny that they had to be newlyweds.

Linda put down her empty martini glass and said, "Oh dear, think I might be getting seasick. I feel kind of dizzy."

"We haven't even left the harbor yet."

Linda put a hand to her head and before you could say *Man overboard*, she'd slid off her barstool and was lying in a heap on the floor.

CHAPTER 2

She was a blonde – with a brunette past.

— GWYN THOMAS, WELSH NOVELIST

For a second, all the occupants of the bar stools stared at Linda, collapsed on the deck.

"A doctor," Toni yelled, recovering from her shock. "Somebody get a doctor!"

On the edge of her vision, she saw Romeo lose the Good Time Charlie act and grab a phone she hadn't even noticed behind the bar.

She threw herself to the ground beside her mother, trying to remember everything she'd learned in that CPR course she'd taken when Tiffany was young, but her mind was blank.

Tiffany, luckily, was made of sterner stuff. She dropped to Linda's other side and immediately put her ear to Linda's mouth. "She's breathing," she said.

"We should do CPR."

"I'm pretty sure her heart's beating."

They stared at each other. Toni had no idea what to do and Tiffany didn't seem to, either. "Mama? Mama! Can you hear me?"

After a moment, a man's shoes appeared in her vision. They were black and had rubber soles, presumably for walking on a ship's deck. "Who called for a doctor?"

Toni glanced up, relief making her almost dizzy, to find a white-haired man wearing an officer's uniform above the black shoes, looking down at her through thick glasses. He was carrying a black medical bag. It reminded Toni oddly of the plastic one Tiffany used to play with when she was a kid.

"You're the doctor?" He looked awfully old to be practicing medicine.

"Doctor Madsen."

"Here, Doctor," Tiffany said urgently, and the doctor took her place kneeling beside Linda.

He seemed to take ages locating his stethoscope in his bag. Then he took another age to fit the earpieces to his ears. Finally, he bent closer to Linda and listened to her heart. "Good, strong beat," he said.

He took her pulse. Looked at his watch. He had to bring the watch to about three inches from his eyes to be able to read it. He nodded.

Letting the stethoscope hang around his neck, he pulled a penlight from the bag. Then he lifted one of Linda's eyelids and shone the light into her eye. He let the eyelid drop again.

"How many drugs has your mother had today?" he asked Toni.

Obnoxious old coot. Her impressive chest swelled with indignation as she said, "My mother is not on drugs."

When Linda had collapsed, she'd taken her purse down with her and it lay beside her, a scatter of her belongings spilling out. Tiffany picked up what was left of the blister pack of travel medication. Nearly all the pills were gone. She held it out to the doctor, who merely nodded once more. "She overdosed on Dramamine and mixed it with alcohol. I've seen it countless times. Your mother will be fine. She simply needs to sleep it off."

It took two strong young stewards to hoist Linda back to their stateroom. They laid her down tenderly on one of the beds and Linda groaned, then turned on her side, muttering something.

Okay, not the start to the cruise she'd have imagined, but Toni always liked to look on the bright side. While Linda slept off her Dramamine bender, she and Tiffany could enjoy some quality mother-daughter time. "I think we should start our cruise with a tour of the salon and spa."

A pained groan met her words. "No. Don't make me."

"Honey, it's right beside the gym. We'll tour the spa, then we'll check out the machines and weights. And Grandma can enjoy her nap in private." In truth, her mama was flat on her back snoring like a stevedore with bad adenoids. She wanted to get her daughter out of the room before she suffered hearing loss.

The pair of them had barely reached the spa, where the heavenly smells of aromatherapy greeted them, along with the almost spiritual hush common to all good spas, when a woman in a brown suit and a brass nameplate pinned to her breast bustled up to them. "Yes, can I help you?" she asked in a singsong voice. Her nametag announced that she was Lorna from Jamaica.

"Yes. We'd like a tour of the spa, please," Toni said, already checking to see what, if any, cosmetics the spa carried. None that she could see, which was very good news to a woman who hoped to introduce as many of the *Duchess* cruise passengers as possible to the benefits of Lady Bianca cosmetics.

Naturally, there was an unwritten etiquette about selling products on a cruise ship. Generally, it was frowned upon unless it was one of the sanctioned products or services offered by the cruise ship company itself.

However, a woman didn't sit in the Lady Bianca platinum circle (and have the ring to prove it) without learning how to talk about her job in a way that left women plenty of opportunity to ask her more. If they didn't, that was fine. But any interest at all and Toni would be only too willing to bring her bag of Lady Bianca products into their stateroom and offer a free facial and makeup application lesson.

"Certainly." The woman called over a young woman in a similarly colored brown smock. "Megan will be happy to take you ladies on a tour."

"Mom, check this out."

She turned and found her daughter regarding a table setup advertising medi-spa treatments. *Go home refreshed*, the poster board said. There was a list of treatment options from dermabrasion to injections to erase wrinkles, to fillers and collagen treatments. But what had Tiffany staring was the photograph that went along with the advertising. Dr. Madsen was the specialist. "He can barely see! Imagine letting him near your face with a hypodermic full of poison," Tiffany whispered before they were joined by their tour guide.

Megan nodded and smiled at them and said, "We offer all the services of a top spa."

And Toni sighed in bliss. Spas and salons were among her favorite places on earth and she spent a happy half hour breathing in lemongrass and ginseng, poking her nose into vapor steam rooms and testing out the hot stone lounging beds. She learned all about the signature facials, the hot stone pedicures, the rejuvenation body work; she could even get her teeth whitened and her wrinkles plumped without ever leaving the comfort of the ship. She happily accepted a color brochure detailing all the salon services, knowing she'd be back. And soon.

"If you'd like to book now, you'll avoid the crowd."

Before Toni could answer, her attention was caught by the sound of moaning. She glanced up to see a woman walking past, her head down, holding an ice pack to her lip. Her upper lip was the approximate size and shape of the starship *Enterprise* and obviously painful.

"Did Dr. Madsen do that?" Tiffany asked, staring after the woman.

A thin smile greeted her words. "That was most likely an allergic reaction. It's very rare. May I book you in for a consultation?"

"Maybe later. I think we're ready to see the gym."

Toni had a different relationship with the gym than she did with the salon. Toni looked forward to the spa the way she looked forward to visiting a close friend, to hours sharing girl talk, maybe painting each other's toenails and watching a chick flick. The gym was more like an acquaintance you never really liked who was going through a hard time and so you felt obliged to visit, even though you knew every minute would be misery.

Her daughter, strangely, felt the exact opposite way about both places. Naturally, Toni was delighted that her daughter enjoyed athletic pursuits and spent time keeping her body in good physical condition. She only wished she shared a little bit of her mother's pleasure in makeup and facials—who could resist the pedicure with the lemon ginseng salt scrub and hot stone massage? Or the therapeutic and oh, so decadent hydrating facial that promised smoother, plumper, and more lustrous skin.

When they entered the fitness center, they were greeted by the ominous sounds of clanking weights. The air was scented with the much less aromatherapeutic smell emanating from a dozen gym rats hard at work. Toni wanted to retreat back to the spa with the soothing sounds of waterfalls and panpipes and the scents of lavender and lemon.

The fitness center was well laid out, with rows of treadmills, stationary bikes, and elliptical machines all facing the view out of the enormous windows where the sea sparkled and other ships stacked up near them like ocean-going skyscrapers. A young guy, late teens, maybe early twenties, stood in the mat area clearly taking a short break. Sweat pebbled his face and he was breathing heavily.

She'd have paid him no more attention except that beside her, she felt the air shift. She glanced at her daughter and caught her staring at him and then looking away with studied nonchalance.

Suddenly, the young guy's break was over. He bent forward and dropped so his hands rested on a low bench like the kind

Toni had used when she used to take a step class, then he hooked his feet over a large green exercise ball so he was in a push-up position. From that unlikely pose, he launched into a set of aggressive and very impressive push-ups. Maybe her daughter was pretending not to be interested but Toni couldn't stop staring. How fit would you have to be to balance your feet on a ball and do push-ups while on a slightly moving ship?

"And we also offer yoga, spin, Zumba classes, and of course a package with our personal trainers," their tour guide said.

"What's Zumba?" Toni asked, tearing her gaze away from the young bodybuilder.

"It's a dance-based workout. It's really fun. I promise you won't even know you're exercising."

"Oh, believe me, I'll know it." But still, *dance based* had to be good.

"What are the gym hours?" Tiffany asked.

"Six o'clock in the morning until ten at night."

With a slight thud of athletic shoes hitting the deck, the boy straightened once more. He strode past them, heading deeper into the gym and swaggering past her daughter. "How's it going?" he asked Tiffany.

She raised both hands and pushed her dark hair behind her ears. "Okay," she said.

He nodded and moved on.

So much for the mating rituals of the young.

When they arrived back at the reception area and had thanked their guide, Toni suggested that she and her daughter get some green tea and settle in a couple of loungers.

It was nice to sit out on the deck, enjoying the sunshine

and the company of her daughter. They didn't talk much, but it was an easy silence. She began to think that the three of them coming on this trip was a great idea.

After half an hour or so, she headed back in search of more green tea. But the woman in the brown suit shook her head. "You have to go to your muster station now," she said. "The safety demonstration begins in a few minutes and you can't miss it. Go to your staterooms, pick up your life jackets, and proceed to your muster station."

"Where is our muster station?"

The woman checked Toni's cruise card and told her to report to the Duchess Theater five floors below.

When they arrived back at their stateroom, they found Linda groggy but awake.

"How are you feeling, Mama?"

"Like I've been ridden hard and put away wet."

"We need to take our lifejackets and go to the theater for a safety demonstration."

Linda sat up, looking leery. "What kind of safety demonstration? Isn't it safe on a cruise ship?"

"Of course it is," she hastened to reassure her mother before she could pop any more pills. "But we will be at sea. This is merely a safety precaution."

They gathered up the three red lifejackets from the top shelf of the closet. Linda pulled open the small fridge in their stateroom, found one of the bottles of water, upended it, and drained it dry. "Okay, let me fix my hair and makeup and I'll be ready." Since Linda was wearing one of her many fake hairpieces, and it had become slightly dislodged by her nap, Toni suspected they'd be waiting for a while.

Luckily, the ship personnel were obviously well accustomed to their patrons taking a little extra time to get ready. At every turn down the stairs they encountered a crew member wearing a life vest identical to the ones the women carried, a bright green ball cap, and a determined smile, as they checked cards and ushered them toward their muster station.

The emergency meeting place for Toni's suite was the Duchess Theater, where events from Broadway-style musicals to comedy shows to afternoon movies would appear for their entertainment. "My gosh," Linda said as they entered the theater, gazing around her. "This theater's almost as big as the Grand Ole Opry."

That was a bit of an exaggeration, but it was indeed a large theater, built on two levels. It probably seated a thousand people. The décor was rich with red upholstery, polished wooden rails, and mirrored walls etched with the Duchess logo. They were directed into rows by uniformed crew, as though they were cars being parked. Then they settled, each holding her life jacket like a stuffed animal on her lap.

They probably waited ten more minutes for the rest of the passengers to arrive at their muster station. They were every age, every color, most in colorful garb, and all determined to have a good time.

A man wearing an officer's uniform took the stage, wearing his life jacket. "Welcome aboard, ladies and gentlemen," he began. Then he explained how important safety was to the company and the crew, calling it their top priority, which Toni was very relieved to hear. She couldn't imagine how she'd feel if she got on a ship, and they said, *Good afternoon, we take your safety pretty lightly. Let's face it, there are thousands of passengers on board. Who'd really miss a couple of you?*

"We will now demonstrate how to put on the life jacket." Various crew members moved to the aisles, all of them already wearing their life jackets. They mimed putting the jackets on, indicated how the straps could be tightened, showed where the whistle was and pointed to the light that would illuminate "should you enter the water."

Beside her, Linda's chin dropped closer to her chest and soon her mother was once more napping. Toni didn't think she was missing anything too important, so she let her sleep. The man at the front described the evacuation procedure, which was basically not to panic and to do what the crew told you. To grab your life jacket and not to abandon ship until given the order to do so.

"Don't worry," she mumbled.

"And now, should you ever hear seven short blasts followed by one long blast of the whistle, that is the call to the emergency muster stations. If you hear this whistle, do not panic. Get your life jacket and come back here. You will now hear the emergency signal."

While they sat there in the comfort of a two-level theater, soft in their upholstered seats, seven short whistle blasts sounded.

"What's that?" Linda asked, jerking awake.

"The emergency whistle," the woman on her other side informed her.

"Oh, my God," Linda screamed and grabbed at her life jacket, unclipping the strap, which was stubborn and didn't want to unclip.

"It's just a drill, Mama," Toni said. "Not for real."

"Well, thank heaven for that. I can't even get the buckle undone."

She grew even more distressed as the crew explained how to hold down the jacket with one hand while pinching the nose and covering the mouth with the other. "Then don't jump in the water," they were told. "Simply step forward."

"Are they out of their minds? Step forward off the side of this ship? Have you seen how tall this ship is? It would be like stepping off Mars."

The drill ended with an offer that if anyone wanted to practice putting on their life jackets, the crew would help them.

Linda's life jacket was a bit of a mess, so Toni said, "Let's try getting that on you, Mama, so we know it works."

Linda had managed to get the clip undone. Now she pulled the two front pieces apart, and Toni heard the rip of Velcro, then she pulled it gingerly over her hair. She'd gone with one of her elaborate Dolly-Parton-is-my-hero hairpieces this morning, so platinum ringlets danced and fought as she did a kind of Mambo, twisting her head one way and the life jacket the other, until it was over her head. At last, they had her head in and as Toni pulled the straps tight around her mother's body, she pushed the clip pieces together. Now she knew why the crew demonstrated how to put on a life jacket while already wearing one. It was not easy to get these things on.

As the buckle clicked home, her mom yelled, *"Ow."*

A uniformed crew member, clearly seeing a real emergency, stepped forward to help.

"This jacket is so small an anorexic toothpick wouldn't fit inside," she gasped, fighting for breath.

"Here, madam, let me help you." The young man was in his mid-thirties probably and had the kind of ethnicity that could be a mix of a hundred histories. He was gorgeous, with high cheekbones, big brown eyes, white teeth, and dark curly hair.

"Thank you," Linda wheezed, gazing into his beautiful face. "These things are not designed for a well-endowed woman." Not that she really had to tell him that. Her breasts had been flattened by the life jacket and with nowhere to go but up, they spilled from the top of the red life jacket like escapees from a boob prison.

Toni really, really hoped they didn't have to don one of those things and abandon ship.

Linda flapped her arms. "Get me out of this thing." She was part panicked, part still high on Dramamine and cocktails, and part enjoying the attentions of the young, handsome steward.

As he unclipped her, he tried to ease the life jacket over her head while she pulled and yanked her head out. Toni had no idea how it happened, but next came a yowl of pure pain. "My hair. Oh, ow, my head."

The young man, probably thinking she was having some kind of medical emergency, abandoned all attempts to ease the jacket off her. He dragged the jacket off the screaming Linda, and to Toni's horror, as he pulled, a couple of the platinum ringlets caught in the Velcro. The life vest came off, taking Linda's hairpiece with it. About fifteen wayward platinum sausage curls trailed from the red jacket.

She had no idea how many years of training the poor guy had, but he took one look at the head of hair hanging suspended from the jacket and, with a cry of horror, flung the jacket away, so it flew through the air.

Linda, meanwhile, was grasping at her head, clutching the front part of her hairdo, which still looked perfect thanks to about half a can of hairspray and careful backcombing, but the back end of her head looked as though she'd stuck her entire head into an electrical socket.

The disembodied hairpiece, meanwhile, hanging out of the life jacket like a guillotine victim, sailed across the aisle and into the next row. It landed in a woman's lap and she screamed, "Oh my God, it's alive. Kill it!"

There were approximately a thousand people in the theater, all of whom had spent the last half hour discussing emergencies; they were collectively a little on edge.

At the woman's scream, a huge man with tattooed arms and a buzz cut grabbed the life-belted hairpiece, threw it to the floor, jumped up, and stomped on it with thick black leather boots. Then, making sure of his kill, he ground the hair under his heel.

For the second time that day, Linda Plotnik made a sound like a moan and fell to the ground.

CHAPTER 3

Whenever I feel like exercise, I lie down until the feeling passes.

— ROBERT M. HUTCHINS

Somehow, they got Linda back to their cabin, with an honor guard of attendants still wearing their fluorescent green ball caps and bright red life jackets, complete with dangling red whistles.

Linda was laid down tenderly on her bed once more. And Dr. Madsen was once again paged.

"Well," the jovial old man said, peering up and down and then finally looking right over the top of his glasses. "Damn trifocals," he said to no one in particular. "Can't get used to 'em."

He picked up Linda's wrist and once more calculated her pulse. He listened to her heart and asked her a few simple questions like what day it was and her name. She aced the test, luckily. And at least this time she was conscious, so Toni was less worried.

"Well, it's not often that I get called twice in the same day to the same patient," he said, sounding pleased to be useful.

"And we haven't even left the dock yet," Tiffany said, like the voice of doom.

"Your grandmother will be fine. She's had a shock, that's all." He looked at Linda.

"Thank you, Doctor. It was a shock."

He patted her shoulder. "Try to get some rest. You'll be as good as new in the morning."

Toni walked him to the door. He paused there. "Normally, I'd give her a mild sedative, but with all the Dramamine still in her system—" He shrugged. "—she'll probably sleep through the night. If you're worried about her, there's a doctor on call twenty-four hours a day. One of my colleagues will assist you."

"Thank you, Doctor."

When she returned, Linda was already closing her eyes.

A few minutes later there was a knock on the door. Tiffany crept forward and opened it and their personal steward stood there with a silver tray. On the tray was what was left of Linda's hairpiece.

"It looks like roadkill," she whispered to her mother. "What do I do?"

"Hide it," she whispered back, knowing there weren't enough tranquilizers on board to calm her mom down if she saw what they'd done to her hairpiece. Toni decided to take the ill-treated hair to the salon tomorrow and see if the on-board stylist could fix it.

Tiffany stashed the hair in her school backpack. Then she walked in and looked at her two roommates. "When you told me this trip would be a real adventure, I thought you were joking."

LINDA WOKE up refreshed the next morning and no one made any mention of the mutilated hairpiece. Fortunately, she'd brought almost as many with her as she'd brought pairs of shoes, so she was back in all her platinum glory well before breakfast.

Linda was also full of plans. Each night a newsletter was delivered to their cabin outlining the next day's activities. They were motoring to a private island in the Bahamas, their first port of call, but today was a day at sea. "So many activities. So many ways to reach three thousand potential customers."

Toni shook her head. "There are another fifteen hundred people working on board. That's a pool of forty-five hundred future Lady Bianca customers."

Linda glanced over at Tiffany. "This is why your mom wins all the prizes. She sees the big picture."

Tiffany looked up from her book. "I wish I could see the wall in my room at home."

"What do you think would be fair, Toni? Should we split the boat into sales territories? You work one part and I work another?"

"Sure."

"Tiffany? Do you want a territory?"

"I'm Switzerland."

"Huh?"

"She's neutral, Mama. She means she's staying out of it."

Linda shook her head at her granddaughter. "One day, honey, you'll be in the business. It's in your blood. You should embrace your destiny."

"Gang members probably say the same thing to their kids."

Since Linda was as used to Tiffany's unfortunate attitude to Lady Bianca as Toni was, she pretended she hadn't heard. "Well, let's see." Linda pulled out a map of the ship. "Would y'all look at this? There are sixteen floors to this ship. How do we split up the territories? I mean, how would you even know if the person you were talking to had a stateroom on deck five or deck fifteen?"

She turned the map. "Then there's fore and aft and port and starboard. I'm already dizzy."

"What about trying a team approach?" Toni suggested. "We'll work together and split the new recruits down the middle."

Tiffany glanced up, amusement sparkling in her pretty eyes, but for once she didn't say anything.

"Well, obviously not split the *recruits* down the middle, because that would be messy and unproductive, but if we have let's say two thousand people sign up to sell Lady Bianca cosmetics by the end of the cruise, then you'll get credit for a thousand and I'll get credit for a thousand."

"Two thousand new recruits. Can you just imagine?"

"Of course I can, and I always believe that every person I talk to will eventually sign up to sell Lady Bianca."

Linda shook her head admiringly. "It's a gift you have. That's what it is. A true gift."

Toni was having trouble deciding between the blue striped T-shirt with white cotton slacks or the lilac cotton sweater and a jean skirt. In the end she went with the lilac cotton, as it was the Lady Bianca signature color.

"Oh, I almost forgot," she said, digging in her big bag. "I brought us all lanyards so we can hang our key cards around our necks." The ship issued the cards not only to let them into their staterooms, but also to function as ID and to allow them to purchase drinks or items easily aboard ship.

The lanyards were from the last Lady Bianca sales convention and they were mauve. Imprinted in gold on the pale purple ribbon were the words, *Proud to represent Lady Bianca Cosmetics.* "This way, we won't lose our cards or misplace them somewhere."

"Plus, it's a little bit of soft selling," Linda said, accepting her lanyard, slipping her key card into it and hanging it around her neck. She'd been flipping through the daily newsletter outlining the day's events. Suddenly, she put a hand to her chest and cried out, "Oh, look at this! A shopping seminar. And it's about diamonds and jewelry." She gasped. "And they're giving out prizes."

"Perfect. Women who love diamonds—and who doesn't? —will love Lady Bianca. And by the time they've finished an hour-long seminar on shopping, they'll be pumped to buy. This is a golden opportunity."

"Or a diamond one," Linda said, and the pair of them started giggling.

"Okay, Betty and Wilma, I'm heading for the gym," Tiff said, grabbing her card. She was already in shorts and an athletic shirt, her hair tied back in a ponytail. "I'll catch up with you both later."

"Wow. Aren't you committed to fitness," Linda said admiringly.

Toni watched as her daughter mumbled something and headed for the door. Toni wasn't sure it was a commitment to fitness so much as a desire to bump into the cute young guy from yesterday.

She noticed that Tiffany hadn't taken advantage of the Lady Bianca lanyard.

"Let's start with the Zumba class," Linda suggested. "Lots of great women who care about their appearances will be there. Plus, we'll get a workout."

"Deal."

She abandoned the lilac sweater and jean skirt for workout gear and headed for the nightclub where the class was scheduled. The teacher had set up on the stage and by night, the class gym would be the disco dance floor.

While they waited for the class to start, they checked out their fellow classmates for potential Lady Bianca clients. Toni immediately picked out a few likely candidates.

She smiled and moved close to one of them. An older woman, maybe late fifties, with diamonds at her ears, her throat, and on her fingers. Big, gorgeous diamonds. She had a sad look to her and Toni thought maybe she needed a lift— like, say, a free makeover.

"I've never done Zumba before. Mind if I follow you?" she asked the woman.

"I'll try not to lead you astray." She had a New York accent. She was attractive, with frosted hair cut in a sleek bob, and a lean figure.

The music began to boom out of the speakers while the instructor shouted instructions into her mic. Toni had no time to focus on anything but where her feet were supposed to go. It was a fun workout, with pumping music, stepping this way, jiggling that way, and trying not to crash into anyone.

After the class, when the women were all glowing and feeling good about themselves for choosing to exercise off a few calories instead of packing on more at the buffet, Toni turned to the woman who had more diamonds on her body than Toni did, and whose skin proclaimed regular facials and a beauty regime. "I don't know about you, but I'm ready for a coffee or a fruit juice or something after all this work."

The woman immediately agreed, and since Toni's voice had a carrying quality, a fairly large group of women in workout gear decided to join them. They headed outdoors to a covered area with tables and chairs.

"That was so much fun," Toni said to her new friend as they settled side by side.

"Isn't it? Whenever I'm on a cruise, I never miss a Zumba class."

"You've been on a lot of cruises?"

"I've lost count. I love cruising. I'm a Gold VIP cruiser."

A waiter appeared as soon as they sat down. Toni, feeling virtuous from her Zumba workout, ordered a green tea and a large glass of ice water. "Of course," she confided to the older woman she'd befriended, "I really want coffee, but I'm trying to cut down."

"Not me. I need some pampering. I'm having a latte. With whole milk."

There was a gasp from a woman so thin and hard-bodied she must count calories at night instead of sheep.

When she wasn't selling Lady Bianca, Toni loved nosing out people's personal business. So, sensing an interesting story, she said, "Wow. Whole milk? Things must be really bad...?" She left the question mark hanging there. The woman could pick it up or she could leave it hanging. Her choice.

She picked it up and leaned in. "You have no idea." Her eyes pinched with pain. "I was supposed to be on this cruise with my husband. Instead, I'm traveling with my grandson." She sighed sadly. "I have my divorce lawyer on speed dial."

"Oh, no. I'm divorced. I know how tough it is. I'm so sorry."

"This will be my third. I don't think any woman has worse taste in men than I do. I keep dreaming I've found someone who loves me for myself. But so far, it's turned out to be all about the money." And her eyes filled with tears.

Toni's sympathy was immediately roused. "Do you want to talk about it?"

She gave a bitter laugh. "It's an old, old story. About a girl who grows up with a big trust fund and low self-esteem." The lemon water arrived at that moment, placed before them by the efficient staff member uniformed in a blue and yellow Duchess shirt and beige Bermuda shorts. Her nametag announced that her name was Maricel and she was from the Philippines.

The woman took a sip of the lemon water and Toni did the same. "I'm Alicia, by the way," she said, holding out her hand. "I guess if I'm going to tell you my life story, I should tell you my name."

"Toni Diamond. Real nice to meet you."

They shook hands and Toni noticed Alicia's fingernails were painted a pale shade of coral, the manicure so fresh she must have had it done right before they left, if not on board ship.

Across the table, Linda was the life of the party and Toni imagined that sometime in the next half hour she'd casually drop into the conversation what she did for a living. Nothing pushy or overt, but she'd let this group of women know that she was always available for consultations, "complimentary, of course," and that she'd be more than happy to give them a free facial and makeup application lesson.

Alicia sipped more of the ice water with lemon and the efficient Maricel returned with a tray full of the beverages the women had ordered.

Toni accepted her green tea with a cheerful thank-you and then sipped. "Maybe if I try real hard I can make this taste like coffee."

"And maybe if I try real hard, I can time travel backward thirty years and make different choices."

Toni patted Alicia's hand.

"I'm being morbid, I know. But I really thought this man was different."

"What happened?"

In the background, music played, sounding like a Top 40 radio station. The sky was a perfect blue and the ship barely swayed as it chugged along. "The usual. He started working late a lot. All of a sudden he got a personal trainer and put in extra hours at the gym. He watched what he ate. He even bought himself some new clothes suitable for a hipster." She shrugged. "The only thing missing was the neon billboard announcing he was having an affair. So, I snooped into his personal credit card bills. And I found a pretty hefty bill from a jewelry store."

"Such a cliché."

"I know. My birthday was coming up, so I thought, give

the man the benefit of the doubt. And I waited, hoping I was wrong."

"Oh, honey."

She turned to Toni impulsively. "I don't know if you feel this way, but even though I have a jewelry case full of rings and earrings and necklaces and bracelets, I love getting new jewelry."

"Oh, I know how you feel. I am exactly the same way."

"Well, as I'm sure you've guessed by now, when my birthday arrived, my husband did not give me jewelry. He presented me with a brand-new handbag. It was a very nice handbag by one of my favorite designers."

"But he didn't get it at that jewelry store."

Alicia shook her head sadly. "I am such a fool. I even made a special trip to the jewelry store to check whether they sold handbags."

"They didn't?"

"No. They only sold jewelry."

"And I'm guessing the bling wasn't for his mother or his sister?"

"His mother's dead and he doesn't have a sister. What he did have was a new executive assistant. Her name is Sondra with an O. She's thirty-two years old and trained to be an actress. I guess she did such a good job acting like she was crazy about my sixty-two-year-old husband that he bought a front row seat to every performance."

"I'm so sorry," Toni said again. There was nothing like the heartbreak of being cheated on by someone you loved and trusted. Nothing. If Toni lived to be a thousand years old she'd never forget how much Dwayne Diamond had hurt her. "What did you do?"

In Toni's experience, being cheated on brought out two kinds of women. There were the conciliators, the women who suggested marriage counseling and maybe a holiday to try to rekindle the marriage; and then there were the women who treated cheating like it was a huge pair of scissors to a marriage. Their first call when they discovered the awful truth wasn't to the marriage counselor. It was to the divorce lawyer.

She'd never had a chance to find out which group she belonged to. Dwayne had sneaked out like a thief in the night, leaving her with nothing but her infant daughter and his fancy last name.

"First, I called a very discreet private detective agency and had him followed. Then I called my lawyer." Alicia gave a dry chuckle. "The only good thing to come out of this is that it's the same lawyer who drew up the prenup."

Okay, so Alicia was more of a scissors girl. "Well, as heartbreaking as this is, I guess you have to look on the bright side. At least you have a prenup."

"Oh yeah. I seriously think he believed he'd get away with the affair and I'd never find out about Sondra. It was almost comical how passionately he denied that he was cheating. But, of course, I had pictures and the detective's report. So then he tried crying, suggested marriage counseling, thought maybe we should go on a cruise together and rekindle our marriage." She sipped her drink so suddenly Toni suspected she was forcing herself not to cry. "This is the cruise we were supposed to go on."

"Oh, no."

"Oh, yes. After promising me that he had ended it with Sondra, of course, he hadn't. All he'd done was to get her a different job. Maybe he thought that if I knew they weren't working together, I would believe they weren't sleeping together."

"Why do dumb men tell lies to smart women and think they can get away with them?"

Alicia looked at her in surprise. "How do you know that David is dumb?"

"Please. He had you and instead played hide-the-weenie with thirty-two-year-old Sondra with an *O*? All he had to do was genuinely try and make things work with you and you would have forgiven him." In a way, she wasn't talking about Alicia anymore. She was remembering how she'd hoped and prayed that Dwayne Diamond would return after he'd walked out on her and Tiffany. It shamed her to admit it, but she was fairly certain that she'd have taken him back.

She'd recently become reacquainted with Dwayne when he'd got involved in a foolish moneymaking scheme that led to him being arrested for murder. She was pretty sure he'd have been better off if he'd stayed with her. She wasn't big on revenge, but it was reassuring to know that she'd built a good life for herself and Tiffany, enjoyed her own home and a thriving business she loved, while Dwayne was still working as a two-bit country and western singer off the strip in Vegas, still trading on his fading good looks.

She felt a kinship with Alicia. "And what is it about smart women like us that we fall for the dumb, unethical men?"

"I don't think I am smart. I never learn from my mistakes. Do you?"

Toni sipped green tea. "You know, I think I have." She thought about Luke, who was so honest she sometimes wished he'd tell a little white lie just to save her feelings. But he never did. Luke was not the kind of guy who, if you asked, "Do these jeans make my butt look fat?" would tell you that you were the most beautiful woman in the world. He was more likely to tell you to spend more time at the gym and lay off the Twinkies. But he was also one of the most ethical people she knew. In balance, she was willing to accept the brutal honesty that came with the rock-solid morals of the man.

She leaned forward and patted Alicia's hand one more time. "And you will too. Next time."

"I wish I was better at being alone."

"Being alone isn't the worst thing that can happen to a woman."

"Isn't that the truth?"

"But good for you—you came on the cruise anyway."

"I did. And I think that even if my grandson hadn't come with me, I'd have come on my own. I'm fifty-eight years old. It's time I got used to my own company."

Alicia glanced up and her eyes widened even as her face drained of color. She looked sick and scared. "What are *you* doing here?" She sounded like she'd seen a ghost.

"What?"

"Oh my God, speak of the devil."

"I beg your pardon?"

But Alicia wasn't paying any attention to Toni. Her gaze was fixed on something, or someone, on the other side of the deck. "I've got to go. Excuse me." Alicia jumped up so fast her chair lurched back and then she stumbled out of the lounge area toward the stairs and elevators.

She looked as though she were running away.

But why? Who or what had panicked her?

CHAPTER 4

A divorce is like an amputation; you survive, but there's less of you.

— MARGARET ATWOOD

oni looked back to where Alicia had been gazing when she acted as though she'd seen the first wave of the zombie apocalypse, but a large crowd had emerged onto the deck. Men and women, young, old, black, white. She caught a glimpse of a man with white hair disappearing into the fitness center. Had the unlamented David decided to join the cruise after all?

Was he hoping to surprise his wife and lure her back?

From the horrified expression on Alicia's face, Toni didn't think the ship's chapel would be called upon for a renewal-of-vows service anytime soon.

She gazed after Alicia. The woman had been so upset. Toni didn't like to see anyone suffer, but she had a special soft spot for a woman duped and lied to by a charmer. She rose and decided to follow Alicia. She didn't want to be pushy and if the woman didn't want company and a sympathetic ear, then she'd leave her alone. But Alicia had already told Toni that she didn't love being alone.

She'd looked like she could really use a friend.

Toni rapidly followed in Alicia's wake, but she was still learning her way around the ship. She walked through the doors her new friend had passed through and didn't see any sign of her. Ahead was a bank of elevators. Two passengers stood waiting, while four elevators made their leisurely trips up and down. Neither of the passengers was Alicia.

She nibbled her lower lip. It was possible that Alicia had walked right into an open elevator. Otherwise, she'd taken the stairs, or her cabin was on this floor. Toni ran to port—not that she'd know port from her elbow, but a sign indicated she was on the port side. She glanced up the corridor. It was so long you could roll a bowling ball down it and the ball would disappear from human sight before hitting the other end.

She saw several stewards, each with a cart; presumably they were making up staterooms. She glanced up and down. No sign of Alicia. She darted to the other side of the boat, but Alicia wasn't in the long starboard corridor either.

At this point, Toni gave up. If Alicia had taken the stairs, she had no idea which floor she'd gone to. Enough. Nothing terrible was going to happen if Toni didn't find her. Perhaps the woman's grandson was waiting in her stateroom. Or she'd lock herself in and have a good cry and emerge in time for lunch feeling much better.

Toni returned to the coffee group and found her mother

handing out their free makeover cards as though they were playing cards and she was the queen of Texas Hold 'Em.

"Toni, honey." She beamed at her daughter. "I've got Annabel and Deirdre both wanting facials and makeup application lessons at the same time."

Go, Linda!

She glanced at Toni with an appeal, as though it might be an imposition for her daughter to give up her time to help another woman learn how to apply her makeup, when in fact, there was nothing Toni loved more. Especially if it led to a new customer or a home party or maybe even a new rep for the company.

She pulled out her electronic calendar. "Sure, Mama. When were you thinking?"

When the four of them had picked a time that suited them all, they said goodbye and promised to meet again tomorrow for Zumba.

Maybe they only had two takers for their promotional services, but they'd barely started on the cruise. When they were out of sight of the other women, Toni high-fived her mom. "Way to go, Mama!"

"We are going to have so much fun on this cruise."

"Oh, I know it."

"Now, I'm going to shower and then what do you think? Bingo or line dancing?"

"Is that a serious question?"

Linda chuckled. Bingo was a game of pure chance. It couldn't be manipulated or controlled. But line dancing? Linda Plotnik had practically invented it. And Toni, growing up with Linda as a mother and then marrying a country and western singer, was certainly no slouch.

"Do you think Tiffany will want to come?"

Tiffany, like Toni, had grown up line dancing. She and Toni used to step to "Achy Breaky Heart" shortly after she learned to walk. She might try to deny her heritage, but line dancing was part of her DNA, just like Stetsons and a love for cosmetics and bling.

However, when they got back to the stateroom, Tiff wasn't there. "Never mind. If she hears the music she'll be drawn to it, like the sirens to whatshisname."

Toni chuckled. "I think the sirens tried to entice Ulysses and his men to their deaths."

Linda turned and stared at her. "Well, look at you, all smarty-pants. Where did you learn a thing like that?" She wrinkled her nose. "Was it a movie starring Gerard Butler?"

She shrugged. "Probably. Or else I got it from Tiffany."

After a quick shower, they redid their makeup and hair, donned tight jeans with sparkles on the derriere—Toni had never made the mistake of asking Luke whether *they* made her butt look fat—and headed to the Lido deck.

Some women might swoon when they heard classical music. Some might feel the Latin beat in their blood when they got near salsa or tango. But for Toni, the first bars of "Boot Scootin' Boogie" acted like fishing wire attached to her ankles with some gorgeous crooner reeling her in.

Her hips were twitching and her feet were itching before they even hit the deck.

She glanced around and found about a hundred kindred souls. More women than men. A live band had set up on the deck above and half a dozen of the young "activity leaders," as they were called—kids in their twenties who hailed from every corner of the globe and were all cute and high-energy—stood in front of the pool ready to lead the line.

"Amateurs," Linda whispered.

She was right. They wore white tennis shoes.

Toni glanced around and found all the other participants wearing flip-flops, sandals, or sneakers. She and Linda were the only two in bona fide cowboy boots. Linda's were purple with silver stitching. Toni's were green. She'd had the boot-maker add tiny diamonds to the heels. She loved those boots.

She glanced out and the azure sea of the Caribbean winked at her. She was so happy she felt like winking back. Sunshine, a week with her mama and her daughter, no meals to cook, no errands to run. She could relax and enjoy her cruise.

The activity director, who looked barely old enough to shave, and who introduced himself as Ryan from Brisbane, Australia, got things started. He introduced Esme from England and Anna from Serbia. None of those countries were hotbeds of line dancing, but Toni was prepared to be indulgent.

The band broke into a Marvin Gaye song and Ryan and his two helpers launched into step, clapping along with the beat as Ryan yelled, "To the right, to the right, to the right, pause, to the left, to the left, to the left." Then they did some incomprehensible shimmy and added in a cha-cha move.

"This ain't line dancing," Linda announced.

"It sure isn't, Mama."

They followed along for a few more minutes, Linda becoming increasingly ornery. "You think we should say something? Offer to help them out?"

"I think we should have fun and not worry about how good the lessons are."

Linda did her shimmy and cha-cha. "That's hard for me to do. It's like asking a Baptist preacher to sit in a Catholic church and say amen."

Oh, dear. When Linda started getting religious, she was seriously riled. But Toni had no idea what would have become of her mother's dissatisfaction with the line dancing instruction, because an unfortunate distraction occurred.

A woman broke out of the line, glanced around desperately, ran to the side of the boat, bent over the rail, and vomited.

Unfortunately, the wind was blowing toward them.

From the deck below, six people screamed.

"I guess she's seasick," Linda said, looking a little green around the gills.

Toni looked out but the sea was as close to glassy calm as a sea could be. The only way you'd know the ship was moving was by listening to the muted purr of the engines. She doubted that the woman was seasick. "I hope it's not—"

Another dancer broke the line and bolted for the nearest bucket. She hit the receptacle for the used towels and bent forward, retching.

A sun-wizened older woman said in a loud Brooklyn accent, "Oh, my God, it's the Norovirus."

Toni and her mama exchanged panicked glances. "Have you had your flu shot?" Linda asked. "Because I've been meaning to get one and I simply haven't had a chance."

"I don't think a flu shot will protect you from the Norovirus."

"Well, shoot, what will?"

Toni had no idea. She recalled the bulletins she used to get home from Tiffany's school during flu and cold season, though, back when her daughter was little. "I think the best thing you can do is keep washing your hands with soap and water and try not to touch anything."

"What about food? Can I touch food?" Linda looked slightly panicked and gazed longingly in the direction of the all-you-can-eat buffet.

"Of course you can touch the food." The question was, would you want to?

The line dance class pretty much petered out after that. With two of the dancers missing in action, the punch seemed to go out of the line. Within minutes, crew members wearing so much protective gear they looked like aliens arrived with a cart and began cleaning and disinfecting the area.

Toni and Linda consulted the rest of the day's scheduled activities. "There's still bingo," Linda said.

"You go on to bingo if you want, Mama. I think I'll book something at the spa."

"Okay, honey. Wish me luck."

"I sure do." It wasn't that Toni was averse to, say, the seaweed salt scrub or a stress reducing massage, but her primary purpose in heading for the spa was to slip Linda's mangled hairpiece to the beautician and to do a little snooping. The spa was next door to the gym. If she recalled correctly, there was a nice big window wall separating the two facilities and with luck, she'd get a little peek at what her daughter was up to. With a bit of extra luck, her daughter would never know.

But when she got to the spa, she felt like she was entering

the set of a science fiction movie. Guys in blue overalls wearing surgical masks over their mouths and protective gear over their faces patrolled the halls. It took her a second to realize that they weren't carrying intergalactic weapons. They were carrying buckets and mops. "Oh, dear."

Lorna was on duty again. "I'm sorry, ma'am. The spa is closed temporarily."

"Somebody tossed their cookies, huh?"

The woman smiled at her and said, "We should be open again after lunch."

"Okay. I'll come back," she said, hoping she'd brought enough hand sanitizer with her.

Since it looked to Toni, peeking surreptitiously down the hall to the big window, that the gym was sparsely populated, and there was no one there resembling her daughter, she gave up and headed back outside through the heavy doors. She settled into a nearby lounge chair.

She had no idea how she was supposed to encourage women to feel good about themselves and enjoy complimentary makeup lessons and facials if they were all worried about getting sick.

Toni was a big, huge believer in the power of positive thinking. That every cloud held a silver lining, that when a door slammed in your face, somewhere a window opened. She gazed out to sea, happy that the Lady Bianca prize had been for a balcony suite. At least they could sit outside and smell the fresh sea air.

She grabbed a notepad from her bag, as was her habit whenever she was stumped by something. She wrote, *How can I turn the Norovirus into a Good Thing?*

Nothing sprang to mind.

She tapped her lilac pen against the paper. Then she underlined what she'd written.

She tried brainstorming. She tried the Snowflake Method, a recent addition to her sales toolkit, where you put your big thing in the middle and added linked items out to the side so the resulting diagram looked like a snowflake.

Actually, Toni's never did. Her diagram always looked like a big mess of scribbles, but sometimes she'd light on something fresh. So, she wrote *Norovirus* in the center of a blank page.

She drew a line extending from that circle. *People sick.*

Another line. *Make them feel better?*

She tapped her pen. She wasn't a medical professional or a faith healer. She drew another line.

Once they start to feel better, they will want a treat and new makeup will make them look better.

Oh, now she was on a roll. Of course, it wasn't while passengers were ill and confined to their cabins that they'd want to know about Lady Bianca, it was as they started to improve. She knew for herself that the times she was most likely to buy a beauty treatment were when she'd been sick and was feeling better or when she'd finished a project and felt she deserved a reward. Or, like now, when she was on vacation.

She nodded. All was not lost. Those who weren't sick would be as likely to take an interest in their appearance as before. But those who did fall ill would surely appreciate a little boost when they were back to normal.

Yep, there was that window opening wide and letting in a nice breeze with the scent of the Caribbean. All she and Linda and Tiff had to do was make sure they didn't get sick.

She was busy making plans when an angry female voice broke into her reverie.

"I am going to kill her!"

CHAPTER 5

And I'm never, never sick at sea!
*   What, never?*
*   No, never!*
*   What never?*
*   Hardly ever!*
*   He's hardly ever sick at sea!*
*   Then give three cheers, and one cheer more*
*   For the hardy Captain of the Pinafore!*

— GILBERT AND SULLIVAN (H.M.S. PINAFORE)

*T*oni glanced up to see the bride they'd glimpsed when embarking that first day. She looked seriously pissed and her attendants fluttered around her like newly hatched butterflies trying out their wings.

"How could she do this to me?" the woman ranted.

"I'm sure the beautician didn't mean to get sick," a frightened looking redhead said, glancing at the cloudless sky and pulling on a big sun hat.

The bride turned on her and raised a finger. "My wedding has to be perfect!" she yelled. "Per-fect!"

"I'm sure she'll feel better in time to do the makeup for the wedding."

The bride made a sound like a motorcycle engine sputtering and said, "I'm going to the main deck. I need a hot tub."

She stomped toward the main deck and her attendants fluttered behind and around her.

Doors shut and windows open, Toni reminded herself as she slapped her notebook closed and ran to the nearest changing room, where she slipped into her bikini. It was brand new. Her mother had talked her out of the one-piece and into the much sexier bikini, saying, "I'm wearing a two-piece and I'm your mother. For heaven's sake, girl, you work out, you have a great body. Enjoy it while it lasts."

She'd modeled it for the brutally honest Luke. "What do you think?" she'd asked.

He'd told her to turn around slowly, checked her out from every angle, then walked forward and showed her in his own way that he approved.

She smiled at the memory as she slathered sunscreen all over her exposed skin. Then she followed the bridal party to the central deck, where the big swimming pool sparkled, surrounded by four swirling hot tubs.

In the first was a group of big guys, mostly bald or with close-shaven heads. They looked as though they'd been in the hot tub all morning, slouching out for more beer and then climbing back in again. As they sat, draped over the sides, mostly unmoving, they looked exactly like the sea lions at the aquarium.

This was the busiest part of the ship. It was where you could usually find a live band or something showing on the enormous outdoor movie screen, where the entertainment directors offered contests and dance parties, and the wait staff were kept busy with drink orders.

She spotted the bridal party in the second of the hot tubs, taking up most of the room. But all the hot tubs were pretty full so Toni headed on over, slipped out of her flip-flops and climbed into the heated, bubbling water. "Oh, my," she said. "That feels so good."

The ill will emanating from the bride had flattened her companions. She glared at Toni as though this were her personal space and intruders were not welcome.

"I'm Toni," she said brightly.

"Hi," the nervous redhead said. She had the kind of curly hair and innocent face that made you expect her to break into "The Sun Will Come Out Tomorrow." She glanced at the bride as though making sure it was okay that she'd spoken.

Toni gave the miserable bride the benefit of the doubt, knowing that losing her makeup artist so close to her wedding day was a huge blow. Luckily, she planned to be the fairy godmother to this fairytale wedding, so she continued brightly, "And if I'm not mistaken, you're getting married, isn't that right?"

They all stared at her as though she had superpowers.

She grinned at them. "I saw y'all on the first day. You looked so cute in your matching outfits. And you were wearing a veil, so I figure you must be the lucky bride."

"Unlucky bride." She scowled.

Finally, the redheaded girl who'd managed to say, "Hi," spoke up again. "I'm Lauren, this is Susanne." She indicated a dark-haired woman beside her wearing large sunglasses. Toni thought she might be a couple of years older than the rest of the girls. "And Allie—" Another brunette, with long dark hair in a sloppy bun. "—and Rose." Rose had short, dark hair that was going spiky with the humidity. "And the bride is Caitlyn."

"Pleased to meet y'all."

Caitlyn was full-on blonde and Toni wondered for a moment whether she'd chosen four brunette bridesmaids and a redhead deliberately, so she'd stand out. The bride was very pretty, with big blue eyes, a cascade of blond hair, and clear skin. But her pouty lips were the result of actual pouting and if she wasn't careful, that scowl would give her nasty wrinkles as she aged.

"Where are y'all from?"

Lauren, who seemed to be their spokesperson, said, "We're all from New York except for Allie. She's from Miami."

"And you?" Rose asked her when no one else bothered.

"I'm from a town that's really a suburb of Dallas. I'm Texan born and raised, Rose."

The woman blinked. "You remembered my name?"

"Sure. I remember all your names. In my work it's important for me to memorize people's names and faces."

"You a teacher?"

"No, honey. I'm an independent beauty consultant." They stared at her so she stretched the truth only the tiniest bit. "A makeup artist."

Caitlyn had been staring into the bubbling water, brooding, but her head came up at that. "A makeup artist? Seriously?"

"Uh-huh."

The women all stared at each other and back at Toni.

"You ever done weddings?" Caitlyn pressed her.

She laughed. "Only about a hundred times."

But Caitlyn wasn't one to accept a gift horse without looking it in the mouth, or, in this case, studying its makeup job. Since Toni never, ever went out in public without full makeup on, she was happy to be scrutinized. As she was always reminding her sales team, their faces were a billboard for their products and services.

In the sudden silence, the bubbling water sounded like Niagara Falls. "Would you be interested in showing us a sample of your work?" Caitlyn finally said. "I might need a makeup artist for my wedding."

Smart girl. Toni approved. She wasn't rushing in to hire an unknown makeup artist, even if she was desperate.

"I'd be happy to. In fact, my mama is with me and she's a makeup artist too. We'd be happy to give all you gals a free makeover. If you like our work, you can hire us to do the makeup for your wedding. If it's not to your taste, there's no obligation."

"Great."

"What day are you getting married?"

"Friday. Day before the cruise ends."

"Oh, that's so funny. That's my daughter's birthday. Friday's going to be a very special day on board the Duchess."

Caitlyn did not look as though sharing her wedding day with Toni's daughter's birthday was a big thrill. "Whatever. After the shore excursion tomorrow. Come to my suite. We'll do it there."

"What are you planning in our suite?" the beefy guy who'd carried the wedding dress on board swaggered up wearing board shorts and carrying a bucket with half a dozen open beers in it. He hefted his solid bulk into the swirling water and offered all the women a beer. Even Toni, which she thought was nice of him even as she turned down the treat.

"Long story, but Toni here might do my makeup for the wedding."

"Cool," he said, sucking on his beer.

Toni felt that the hot tub was getting a little crowded, plus she was overheating, so she excused herself and climbed out.

"I'll see you tomorrow," she said. Caitlyn gave Toni her suite number and they agreed on four o'clock as makeover time.

"I CANNOT BELIEVE how well that snowflake worked," Toni told Linda as they ate lunch in the dining room. It was nice here, calm and quiet. Tiffany had begged to join the group of young people who'd found each other and had decided to eat at the buffet. Toni was fairly certain her buff friend from the gym would be part of the group, but she was only too happy to see her daughter having fun.

She and Linda strategized on the best way to prepare one bride and four bridesmaids for the big day in the most efficient manner. "She's getting married on the second to last day, so we've got some time."

They chatted their way through lunch and then the waiter brought them the dessert menu. Toni put up her hand. "I'm not even opening that."

"The tiramisu is excellent today, ladies," their waiter said. "Coffee?"

Toni groaned. "I have no willpower where tiramisu is concerned. I'm going to have to work out more or I won't even fit in that bikini."

"Zumba," her mother reminded her as they both ordered the tiramisu and coffee.

"And how was bingo?" she asked.

"Well, I didn't win anything, but it was fun. I met some nice people there." She set her coffee cup down. "They offer it every sea day. I might go back."

When they were done, Linda said, "I need to get up on deck. I've been inside all day. I want to rest up for the shopping seminar this afternoon." So, Toni put her wet swimwear back on, resolving to buy a second bathing suit when she had a chance. They brushed their teeth, refreshed their makeup and donned big hats, big sunglasses, and toted bottled water and the books they'd brought with them.

Topside, they headed away from the busiest deck to a quieter spot where they found two deck chairs and settled back to enjoy a sunny afternoon.

Toni was half dozing over her book when a man's voice said, "Didn't I meet you at bingo today?"

Beside her, Linda glanced up. "Why, yes, you did."

He was probably a decade younger than Linda, boyishly handsome still, with short, dark hair and big, dark eyes. He addressed Toni. "I was so excited when I got all the letters that I yelled, 'I won.' Your friend reminded me I was supposed to yell 'Bingo.'"

Toni wasn't going to ruin her mother's image by telling the nice man she was Linda's daughter, not her friend, so she said instead, "Linda's a good person to have on your team."

"Oh, honey," her mother said, all flirty and fluttery.

"I'd like to spend some of my winnings by buying you a drink, if I may?"

"You certainly may." Linda jumped up, then realized she was abandoning Toni. "If that's okay with you?"

"You'd be welcome to join us," the man said gallantly.

"No. Thank you. I've got to the exciting part of my book. I'll keep reading. You two have fun."

And she watched them head to one of the outdoor bars, already chatting with the ease of old friends.

Her daughter was making friends, her mother was being romanced. Toni imagined she'd spend a quiet afternoon alone when a voice said, "May I join you?"

CHAPTER 6

I'm not that good looking. Nobody is that good looking. I have seen a lot of movie stars and maybe four are amazing looking. The rest have a team of gay guys who make it happen.

— TINA FEY

She glanced up, then smiled with pleasure. "Alicia. Yes, please join me."

Alicia slipped off a gorgeous beach cover-up and settled on the lounger recently vacated by Linda. Alicia still looked great in a bikini, even if she was fifty-eight. The woman looked much better than the last time Toni had seen her. In fact, she looked as though she'd come straight from the salon. Her hair was sleek with a fresh blowout and her makeup was flawless.

"I am so happy to see you. To be honest, I was looking for you," she said. "I'm sorry I rushed off like that this morning."

"Is everything okay?"

"Yes. I had a bad moment. I haven't been sleeping that well. I thought I saw—well, it's crazy."

Toni gazed at the woman beside her. "I'd have said you looked like you'd seen a ghost, but in fact, you looked like you'd seen your husband."

Alicia leaned forward as though she were going to say something, and then closed her lips together and shook her head. "Like I said, I haven't been sleeping all that well. I was seeing things. I even checked it out and found out I was wrong. Honestly, I think getting a divorce makes me nuts."

"It makes everybody nuts."

Because Alicia had been on numerous cruises and this was Toni's first time, she asked her new friend for information about the upcoming stops. It was an easy, neutral subject and what Alicia didn't know about cruising probably wasn't worth knowing.

Chattering away, they didn't realize they had attracted attention until a grinning waiter appeared in front of them holding a tray with two tropical drinks on it. The first was a mojito, stuffed with mint leaves and deliciously cold looking. The waiter, Henry from Bulgaria, set the drink down beside Alicia. He said, "The gentleman at the bar sent you this. He wanted you to have something long and cool." He turned to Toni and offered her a long glass of fruit punch with a small triangle of pineapple hanging on the rim. "And his friend said to bring you something fruity, with punch."

The women both stared over at the bar and discovered Romeo, the bartender, grinning at them and giving them two thumbs up. The men who had sent over the drinks looked like they'd already sucked back a few cocktails themselves. Both appeared to be in their mid- to late forties and looked as though they might be on a corporate retreat of some sort. They raised their cocktail glasses in a silent toast to Toni and Alicia.

Her mother, settled cozily beside her bingo buddy, glanced over and sent her a wave. Toni suspected the entire group hunkered around the outdoor bar had had a hand in the flirtatious gesture.

"Why, thank you." She and Alicia toasted each other and then responded to the men's silent toast by raising their glasses in return. Toni sipped her rum punch. "You see? There are lots of nice men still out there. You're a very attractive woman."

Alicia snorted. "Dollars to donuts, he's looked at a copy of *Forbes* and figured out my net worth."

"Why would his friend send me a drink? I'm not rich."

Alicia lost her cynical expression and leaned closer, her lips tilting. "No. But you are fruity, with a punch."

She snorted with laughter. "And you're long and cool."

"Should we go over there?" Alicia asked. "It's been so long since I had any man show interest in me that I've forgotten the protocol."

"No," said Toni. "Let them come to us."

So, they chatted and after a while found their drinks empty. Toni turned, but the two men had gone. "Well, I guess they weren't very interested, after all."

"Or something younger and shinier came along."

Even though she was slathered in sunscreen, she still hesitated to spend too long in the tropical sun. "Listen, I need to get out of the sun."

Alicia glanced at the diamond-encrusted watch on her wrist. "Yes. And I've got an appointment."

"I'll see you at Zumba tomorrow, then."

Alicia hesitated. "I hope so." She settled a hand over her stomach. "Truth is, I'm feeling a little under the weather." She smiled. "But it's probably nothing."

DINNER WAS a big deal on the *Duchess of the Caribbean*. Passengers had the choice of one of two set dinners or they could opt for any time dining, with the idea that you could show up anytime between five-thirty and nine-thirty and be seated. There might be a bit of a wait if a lot of people all showed up for dinner at the same time, but Toni had been assured by the travel agent who booked her trip that it wouldn't be more than a few minutes and that there were plenty of things to do in the vicinity if they had to wait.

Apart from the obvious advantage of flexible dining times, was the added attraction that they'd be dining with different people every night. The maître d' would seat people at tables until they were full. This meant that most nights Toni and Linda, and Tiffany, if she decided to join the family business, could meet and talk to new potential Lady Bianca customers.

They were armed with sample packs of product and free makeover coupons. She couldn't wait to get started.

When they got to dinner that night, a nervous looking Asian woman sat beside Toni. "Hi, I'm Toni."

The woman wore a hospital mask over her face and she smiled and nodded when Toni introduced herself. The woman did not return the favor and introduce herself. When the waiter took her order the response was so garbled that the waiter had to ask her three times to repeat her dinner request. Finally, in frustration, she lifted the bottom part of the mask and snapped, "Fettuccine Alfredo and a Caesar salad."

The woman on the other side of Linda said, "See how there are no salt and pepper shakers on the table? They don't want the passengers touching anything. I was reading all about it on Norwalk.com."

"Are you kidding me? Norwalk.com?"

"Sure. It's a fantastic resource. It tells you which ships have reported the virus, when it happened, and how many people got sick. They also have stories from people who've been through epidemics, as well as tips on prevention. Since the virus often pops up again after they've tried to clean the ship, the site recommends avoiding those ships as the chance of getting sick is so high."

Toni ordered the shrimp dish recommended by their waiter, Emil from Bulgaria, and then leaned across her mother to ask the woman, "Was this ship struck with the Norovirus earlier?"

The woman nodded sagely. Paused to order the surf 'n turf, and then leaned in. "Two cruises ago, they had to come in, they had so many people sick. Then last cruise, a bunch more got sick. Chances were really high we'd get hit."

"Why did you take this cruise?"

She put out her hands in a *What can you do?* gesture. "We booked six months ago. Got a great deal on the price. How could I know this would be the *SS Norwalk?*"

Toni wished the good people at her travel agency had accessed Norwalk.com. She'd have to tell them about it. "So, what are your tips for avoiding getting sick?"

"Don't touch anything another person's touched. Stair rails, elevator buttons. If you go in the fitness center, sterilize your equipment *before* you use it as well as after. Deck chairs, ship rails. Think about it. If a sick person could have touched it, then you don't."

"What about the cafeteria?" She thought of all the spoons that got passed from person to person, the communal bread baskets. There were three thousand passengers on board and half as many crew members. Staying away from germs was going to be a monumental task.

"You watch. By tomorrow? Crew will serve you. There won't be any shared utensils. They'll be posting crew members specifically to make sure you get a good squirt of the hand sanitizer. Not that it will do you any good."

"Why not?" Toni had a small bottle in her purse and a larger one in her suitcase. She'd been sanitizing her hands like crazy since the line dancing.

"Doesn't kill the Norovirus. They put that out to make the passengers feel better. Your best bet is to wash your hands with soap and hot water multiple times a day. For as long as it takes you to sing the Happy Birthday song. Or 'Twinkle Twinkle Little Star.' And try not to touch anything."

"I haven't sung 'Twinkle Twinkle' since you were little, Toni," Linda said. Toni appreciated her finding a silver lining to this crisis.

"This isn't exactly the relaxing, leave-all-your-troubles-at-the-dock cruise I was expecting."

The woman looked resigned. "Be glad it's not Ebola."

"Ebola?" She said it so loud that people at the table behind them stopped their conversation and turned to stare.

"Sure. Last cruise I was on, some poor woman had been

on a plane with someone who nursed someone who'd come in contact with Ebola. She was quarantined for the entire cruise and Belize turned us away."

"Oh, how awful. Is she okay?"

The woman snorted. "She never got sick. She didn't have Ebola. We got an extra sea day, though."

"Wow. I never knew cruising could be so dangerous."

As they left the dining room, Linda said, "I want to go to the casino, but I'm scared to touch anything. Not the cards, not the slot machines, not the tables."

Since her mother was a notoriously bad gambler, Toni realized that another positive thing had come from this outbreak. "Never mind, Mama. Why don't we check out the stage show? We can do that without touching anything."

As they made their way through the hallways toward the elevators, they passed several blue overall-clad crew members delivering trays to the rooms of the afflicted.

"It looks like we've been invaded by extraterrestrials," Linda whispered, oddly echoing Toni's earlier thoughts.

When they got to the elevator, there were eight or ten people waiting. Toni and Linda glanced at each other. "Stairs?"

"Yeah. And don't touch the railings."

She hoped to heaven the seas stayed calm, because she and her mom believed that every night on board a cruise was dress-up night and they had the high heels and gowns to prove it.

One lurch from a rogue wave and they'd be tumbling down the staircase like pins at the local five-pin bowling alley.

CHAPTER 7

Vanity, working on a weak head, produces every sort of mischief.

— JANE AUSTEN

"The Bahamas!" Linda cried, staring out at the mass of land ahead of them. The white sand beaches melted into turquoise seas. From out here on the cruise ship, the island looked green and inviting. "I can't believe we're in the Bahamas. I'm so excited."

Toni was excited too. In fact, even Tiffany seemed pleased at the notion of setting foot on their first island stop.

Linda said, "Let's grab a quick breakfast and then head straight over there. You know, the shopping is supposed to be fantastic. And it's all duty-free!" Linda had attended the shopping seminar and come away an evangelist for duty-free shopping. She was also, as she'd been quick to tell them, the proud owner of a VIP shopping card.

"We have to meet in the Caribbean dining room," Toni

said. She'd read up on their shore excursion in the daily newsletter. "We have to take tenders."

"Tenders?"

"Those are smaller boats that will ferry us to land."

When they got to the Caribbean dining room they discovered that when a large portion of three thousand passengers wanted to do the same thing at the same time, there would be a wait.

They were issued numbered tags as they entered, like at the deli, and directed to sit at round dining tables to wait. The tenders took one hundred people at a time. Toni figured there were a few hundred ahead of them.

A group at their table were discussing the shore excursion they'd booked to go scuba diving. "I wonder if we should have booked something," Toni said.

"But we decided to check out the island on our own. This being the first stop and all. Personally, all I want to do is swim in the Caribbean and walk on the white, white sand."

"And don't forget shopping," Tiff reminded her.

"Well, naturally. I have to look at the jewelry. And the watches."

"This is going to be a very expensive cruise," Tiffany teased her grandmother.

"Nonsense. I have willpower of iron."

Toni's lips twitched but she kept her mouth shut. Who didn't love sparkly jewels? Well, Tiffany, but she was young yet.

Their number was soon called and, after double-checking that they had their cruise cards and ID so they could get back on the ship, they were allowed through. They made sure they had their wallets, plus water, sunglasses, sunscreen, and their hats. They were already wearing their bathing suits under their shore clothes.

They followed the line down to level four and the gangway. Then they climbed aboard a smaller boat that would ferry them to the island.

Once there, they found themselves lining up once more. A gorgeous young man dressed as a pirate and a voluptuous young woman in a low-cut, colorful gown posed with each passenger in turn as the ship's photographer snapped their photos.

"Well, isn't this fun?" Linda said, swiping fresh lip gloss over her lips.

"You won't get that picture without paying for it," Tiffany warned her.

"So what? It will be fun to have a souvenir photo of all of us."

When it was their turn, the three of them posed and Toni thought her mama was right. It would be a fun souvenir. She was so happy they'd been able to cruise together, three generations of kick-butt women.

They headed down the dock and soon discovered that they weren't going anywhere near the beaches, the white sand, or the azure water without going through the shopping area first. Huge signs announced Duty-Free Shopping! in different sizes and with differing numbers of exclamation points. Along the route they were offered samples of rum and samples of rum cake. "Oh, my, that is delicious," Linda said, chewing on the dark cake.

They were offered samples of perfume. "Would you just smell that?"

There seemed to be almost as many salespeople offering

to help you, show you something, treat you to an amazing bargain today only, as there were cruise ship passengers. Since their ship was one of three in port, it was crazy busy.

She felt like a young mother, terrified that Tiffany would wander off somewhere and she'd never find her. But Tiffany stuck pretty close to Toni. It was Linda she had to watch. Her mother acted like a wayward toddler, lured by every colorful, moving object she saw, and there were plenty.

Toni prevented her from buying a massive bottle of rum only by reminding her that they'd be coming back through this way and why carry a heavy burden for the rest of the day?

"Why don't you just remind her that she hates rum?" Tiffany asked.

"Because your grandmother is in the throes of shopping fever. It robs her of all rationality and pretty much guarantees she'll suffer buyer's remorse when she gets her credit card bill."

Tiffany turned pale and grabbed her mother's arm. "It won't be like that time she dragged us to Dollywood, will it?"

Even Toni felt a little light-headed as she recalled the experience of joining her mother in the Dollywood gift shop. Linda's mantel over her electric fireplace and nearly every wall and surface in her mobile home were covered with the souvenirs of that trip. "No. Nothing will ever be that bad again."

However, the best was saved for last. The diamond store, the watch store, and the emerald store sparkled ahead of them. "A whole store for emeralds?" Tiffany asked in a stunned tone.

"I know!" Linda said. "Oh, isn't that necklace absolutely

darling? Errol, my personal shopping consultant, says all real emeralds have faults. They're called *inclusions*. No. Something like that. *Occlusions*. But see what a lovely color that one is? And the way it's surrounded by diamonds to bring out the color and quality of the stone? Toni, you should try it on."

"Mama, it's twenty-two thousand dollars."

"But duty-free!"

When they finally got out of the shopping arcade, with a solemn promise to Linda to leave plenty of time for shopping at the end of the day, they exited the air-conditioned stores into the balmy tropical air.

A steel band was playing somewhere nearby, and the immediate vicinity was given over to promoting excursions or selling food or drink. A huge building with a thatched roof and palm trees out front announced Jimmy Buffett's Margaritaville.

"Oh, look at that." Linda had her camera out and was snapping photos like crazy.

Toni could imagine the entire shore excursion slipping away. "Let's head to the beach and grab us some lounge chairs. I'm dying for a dip in the ocean."

Linda snapped a few more photos.

"Sounds good to me," said Tiffany.

"Oh, look," Linda said, "there's Dr. Madsen."

Toni glanced behind her and sure enough, the doctor was striding down the road outside the shopping arcade. He was dressed in his uniform and carrying his medical bag. In the milling groups of vacationers, he seemed like a man with a purpose and a destination. "I guess he treats passengers even if they get sick on land," Linda mused.

"Did you just take his picture?"

"I want a photograph of the man who saved my life," she said with dignity.

They found, when they got to the gorgeous white sand beach, that there were lounges set, row on row, just like on the cruise ship.

THEY SWAM in the warm tropical ocean, enjoyed a fresh seafood lunch, and then, with both of them chaperoning, allowed Linda back into the shopping center. Tiffany even got into the spirit of the thing, buying a new bikini that reminded Toni that she was blooming into a beautiful young woman.

Toni also splurged on a second bathing suit. "Because there is nothing worse than putting on a damp suit." And Linda came away with a bulging bag of souvenirs. Luckily, they talked her out of the vat of rum, and the emerald case remained undisturbed by the end of their visit, which Toni considered a huge win.

They were back on board by three, and Toni said, "We'd better shower up and get ready, Mama—we've got our meeting at four o'clock." She turned to her daughter. "How about you, honey? Will you find something to do?"

"Oh, sure. I'll probably get cleaned up and head for the pool." Since her daughter had been surreptitiously checking the time on her phone for the past hour, Toni suspected she had some kind of appointment herself.

They showered, dressed, and got their full makeup on. Then they checked their supplies. Even though they hadn't anticipated being called on to do the makeup for a wedding, Toni and Linda had taken seriously the Lady Bianca maxim to prepare for success. Toni had set foot on the *Duchess of the Caribbean* convinced that opportunity lay on board. She'd been right. Though, of course, she couldn't have known what form that success would take. She and Linda were riding to the rescue to save a bride's wedding day and who knew where that would lead?

They found Caitlyn's suite and before they knocked, Toni turned to Linda. "You ready, Mama?"

"Let's kill it," Linda said.

She nodded and then knocked on the door.

It was opened by the redhead.

"Hi, y'all," Toni said as she walked in carrying her makeup case, followed by her mother carrying an identical case. "Who's ready to look gorgeous?"

To her relief, the bride was in a good mood and that had put all her bridesmaids in good moods, too. Half her work was done.

"This is my mama, Linda. We're going to get started right away." Normally, she began with an introduction speech, but her brief acquaintance with Caitlyn made her suspect that the bride would be impatient. She and Linda had strategized that they were better to go off script and get right to the makeovers. They'd drop in the information about the company, the benefits of the products, and the opportunities available as they were working.

Toni set up the bride at the small desk, which had a mirror, while Linda sat Lauren in one of the club chairs. They'd keep going until they'd made over all the girls.

Toni was accustomed to working in front of a group, so she talked nonstop as she worked. Linda was no slouch in the talking department either and, with the silent communication of women who are as close as a mother and daughter, they passed the invisible microphone back and forth flawlessly.

Of course, they didn't want to bore the poor women, so they also made sure to engage them in conversation. "How did you decide on this cruise?" Toni asked.

Caitlyn answered, "I knew I wanted to get married on board a cruise ship. We were all checking them out online and with our travel agents, but Susanne came up with the best deal. You would not believe how inexpensive this trip is. Right, Susanne?"

Toni glanced over to find Susanne watching Linda show Allie how to apply eyeliner correctly.

"Earth to Susanne!"

Susanne jerked and looked up. "Sorry, I was daydreaming. What did you say?"

"I was telling her you got us a great deal." Then Caitlyn laughed. "I bet I'll totally be like that when I'm married. Someone will call 'Mrs. Perkins,' and I'll totally be, like, what? You talking to me?" She laughed heartily and Susanne blushed and laughed along with her. "I was telling Toni what a great deal you got us."

"Oh, yeah. I have a friend who had some pull."

"Wonderful. Isn't it great when you get a screaming good deal?" she said.

The mic passed invisibly to Linda, who said, "We won this cruise." Pause.

"Really? How?" Rose obligingly asked.

"Toni won a cruise for two people because she is the top salesperson with Lady Bianca Cosmetics. You would not believe the prizes and incentives. We've won jewelry, cars, all kinds of things. It's a company that truly empowers women."

Pause as she passed the mic back to Toni.

"That's right. Mama's in the top tier for Texas also. What are you working toward now, Mama?"

"I've got my eye on this darling little Prius. We get to make women look better and we make money." She sighed. "I love my job."

"You can win jewelry too, did I mention that?"

At the mention of jewelry, Toni saw Susanne finger a handsome emerald and diamond ring on her left ring finger. "Did you get that ring at the emerald store today?" If so, it had cost her a bundle, based on the size of the stone and the prices Toni had witnessed. Even duty-free.

"No," Susanne said, smiling down at the ring. Toni knew she'd guessed right. The woman was pleased to be asked. "It's my engagement ring. I'm getting married too."

"Congratulations." Based on the condition of the ring, it was a very recent engagement.

"I know, right?" Caitlyn said. "I told her we should have a double wedding."

And Toni completely understood anyone not wanting to have a double wedding with Caitlyn. She thought she'd rather remain single forever.

"Have you all known each other for long?" She imagined she'd hear the usual bride and her attendants' stories about lifelong friendships.

Caitlyn said, "No. Not really. Well, Allie I've known forever, because she's, like, my cousin, but the rest of the girls are newer friends." She sighed. "I mean, there are girls I've known longer and a couple of them were pretty bummed not to be bridesmaids, but I have to think of my future."

Toni had no idea what to say to that so she kept her mouth shut.

"I mean, I will be looking at the wedding photos for the rest of my life. And some of my girlfriends—" She stared at her own reflection in the mirror as she spoke—"They have really let themselves go."

"You chose your bridesmaids for their looks?" Linda asked.

"Yeah. Doesn't everybody? Rose I know from the gym. We work out together and she's totally into fitness and looking good. Lauren and I work together and we both love shopping. And Susanne's also at my gym. This girl Pilar, also from the gym, was supposed to be my fourth bridesmaid. She's from Peru and has this gorgeous thick, black hair down to her waist. But she got sick. So I asked Susanne."

Toni could easily imagine, if she'd discovered she was a bridesmaid to the bride from hell, that she'd suddenly fall sick too.

At the end of ninety minutes, after Caitlyn had experimented with three shades of eye contouring and insisted on going a darker shade of pink than Toni advised for her lips, Toni and Linda had officially been hired to do the makeup for Caitlyn's wedding. They'd also heard more about the bride than they ever wanted to.

"Do you want to see the dress?" She spoke to Toni and Linda, but she still looked at herself in the mirror, turning this way and that, admiring her own beauty.

"Sure. We'd love to."

Caitlyn remained where she was, studying her reflection

in the mirror. "Allie?" she said, glancing up. "Can you go get my dress?"

"Oh, sure." Allie jumped up and went to fetch the garment bag that Toni remembered from the first day. She also recollected Tiffany's comment that the groomsmen's T-shirts should read *Doom Support* and had to suppress a smile.

Allie carried the heavy bag into the center of the suite and Lauren helped her unzip and carefully remove the wedding dress.

The gown was gorgeous, with multiple tiers and a low bosom. Linda and Toni both raved. Caitlyn stared at the white layers of fabric, biting her lip. "I've eaten so much on board, I should try it on and make sure it still fits," she announced. Toni saw the glances Lauren and Allie exchanged and suspected the bride had used multiple excuses to try on that gown. But Toni understood the impulse. She'd only officially wear the dress once. She wanted to play at being the bride, especially now that her makeup was wedding-day ready. Toni decided to help her out.

"It will also give you a chance to see if you like the color palette you'll be wearing against the tone of the silk." And hopefully common sense would prevail and she'd realize that pink was too bright.

With a determined nod, Caitlyn stood and stripped down to her underwear. She wore a lacy thong and bra set.

All the women gathered around like an experienced pit crew around a NASCAR stock car as it pulls in mid-race. Two of them held the dress and Lauren carefully unzipped the back, while Allie ran to the closet and emerged with white satin pumps and a silk bag. She carefully eased the bag over the bride's head, clearly to protect the dress from soil from makeup or hair product, and then the women helped Caitlyn into the dress. Every breath in the room was held as Lauren zipped her up, but thankfully the dress seemed to fit.

Caitlyn removed the bag, stepped into her shoes, and then turned to the full-length mirror. She did look stunning and her satisfied expression suggested she knew it.

Toni and Linda were quick to gush over how lovely she looked as she turned this way and that, viewing herself in the mirror from every angle. "I better lay off the buffet for the next two days," she announced. And then, "Oh, wait, I totally forgot." And, running to her bureau, she pulled open the top drawer and rummaged through her underwear to emerge with a pair of gel-filled breast enlargement pads.

She motioned to Lauren, who unzipped the dress a few inches. She pushed the pads into the bodice and shifted things around until she was satisfied, then nodded at Lauren to zip her up again.

The result was that her newly plumped breasts all but spilled out of the low bodice, reminding Toni of the covers of the historical romance novels that Linda loved to read, where the demure duchess always seemed to be falling out of her gown under the heated glare of the rakish duke. But Caitlyn seemed happy and that made the rest of them happy.

When Toni and Linda left, they didn't say a word until they were back in their own suite. Then they both collapsed on their beds. "Oh, my gosh. That girl should be on one of those reality shows about scary brides."

"I know. And what about those poor, terrorized bridesmaids?"

"But we got ourselves a nice little job and I can imagine at least a couple of lifetime customers. And maybe a sales rep or two. Who knows?"

Linda picked up the daily schedule of events and turned suddenly to Toni. "I know how we can celebrate."

"How's that, Mama?"

"It's karaoke night tonight, that's how. In the Orchid Lounge, where they had bingo, so I even know how to find it."

Anything that kept Linda out of the casino seemed like an excellent plan to Toni. Linda had decades of experience belting out the entire Dolly Parton song list in the shower, while driving a car, doing her housework—really, every minute she wasn't talking, pretty much, she was singing. There were times when she sounded more like Dolly Parton than Dolly Parton did.

"Sure," she said. "I think karaoke would be fun."

Tiffany joined them in time for dinner, seeming pretty vague about what she'd been doing for the past few hours.

They enjoyed yet another excellent meal, this time at a table with only the three of them, which was actually kind of fun. Linda told her granddaughter about their karaoke plans.

Tiffany said, "Mom, I am only going if you promise me you won't sing."

Since one of Toni's great regrets in life was that she hadn't inherited any of her mother's musical talent, she said, "I promise." Then she grinned. "But you know who should sign up?"

Tiffany was shaking her head before her mom had two words out. "Oh, no. Don't even think about it."

"But you have an amazing voice. It's like you got your grandmother's talent, plus your dad's, and completely bypassed my less than stellar musical abilities."

Toni had heard her daughter play the guitar and sing a few times when she hadn't known her mom was in the house, so she knew that Tiffany was interested. One day, maybe, she'd share her talent with the world. "Okay. I won't embarrass you." Then she added, "At least, any more than I can help."

"I thought there might be a talent night," Linda said, recovering instantly from her Caitlyn-induced exhaustion. "But this is even better. Good thing I brought my costume."

Linda Plotnik did not take karaoke lightly. She dressed in one of her Partonesque gowns, and was well-endowed enough that she certainly didn't need any gel pads to give anyone the idea that if she breathed too deeply her show would spill out into X-rated territory. Her dress was tight-fitting, blue-sequined, and slit up the side. She wore her most elaborate hairpiece, the double-thick false eyelashes, and she made the most of having an entire suitcase full of cosmetic products at her disposal.

When she emerged from the bathroom, all ready for her big appearance, Tiffany cheered. "You are hot, Grandma."

Toni wondered why, if she herself wore one sequin, her daughter shrank away in embarrassment, but her grandmother could corner the entire sequin market and plaster it over her body and Tiffany cheered.

They left themselves extra time, since between the height of her heels and the tightness of her dress, Linda could only take small steps. "You sure you can sing in that thing?" Toni asked as they approached the Orchid Lounge.

"I have to put on my best costume and my best show. This might seem like amateur hour to you, but a lot of former show people love cruising, you know. Plus, the grand prize is a thousand dollars."

"A thousand bucks? For karaoke?" Tiff seemed amazed.

Toni glanced at her. "You sure you don't want to give your grandmother some competition?"

"So sure."

They entered the lounge and found it surprisingly full. Two of the cruise entertainment directors were on hand, a young woman and Ryan from Brisbane, who'd been in charge of the line dancing.

Linda saw him too. "If they do a talent night on board," she announced, "We are going to demonstrate line dancing." She glared. "As it *should* be performed."

Since she was an excellent dancer, Toni was happy to agree.

A number of people were already in line to sign up for the karaoke. Toni wasn't certain if it was the money or the chance to show off their skills that had them thronging to put their names down, but she suspected it would be a fun evening.

While Linda headed to the front, she and Tiffany found a table with a great view of the floor. When Linda returned, Tiff said, "I was checking out your competition, Grandma. You should take it on stage presence alone."

"Why, thanks, honey."

"Though I would worry about the Tom Jones lookalike at three o'clock. I totally think he's wearing a hairpiece on his chest."

CHAPTER 8

I never forget a face – but in your case I'll make an exception.

— GROUCHO MARX

araoke started right on time. Skimpily clad waitresses strolled among tables taking drink orders, and ship passengers wandered in and out of the lounge, but there was a hardcore group gathered, like Toni and her family, in the best seats. They were the performers, friends and family of the performers, and people who obviously loved watching karaoke.

"Welcome, everybody, to our karaoke competition!" Ryan from Brisbane boomed, sounding so excited to hear a bunch of amateurs sing songs he'd probably never heard of that he could hardly stand it.

Everybody clapped as he introduced himself and his "lovely co–entertainment director, Kimberly Martin from London, England!"

Kimberly then took over. "Now, let's get started right away. We've got Mr. Nigel Waterford on first—come on up."

It took Mr. Nigel Waterford a while to come on up since he was about a hundred and twelve years old and needed the help of his equally aged wife to get him and his walker up on stage. But he was a game performer.

"I bet he performed on the Titanic," Tiff whispered as he cleared his throat and accepted the mic.

"And what are you going to sing for us, Mr. Waterford?"

"I'm going to sing, 'Thank Heaven for Little Girls.'"

"Good choice for an aging voice," Linda said. She never made the mistake of discounting her competition because of initial impressions.

The music came up and it was soon clear that Mr. Nigel Waterford was too nearsighted to read the prompter. It didn't matter. Toni had seen the movie countless times growing up, where Maurice Chevalier talked/sang the words, and since Mr. Waterford was probably the same age Maurice Chevalier would be if he were still alive, he clearly knew the song inside out.

He didn't follow the prompted words, but his rendition was close enough to the music that it didn't matter. He was an old charmer and when he was done, the applause was thunderous.

Linda looked worried. "You always have to watch out for the sympathy vote," she said.

The second performer was called up on stage. She was a tiny woman with a bad perm who sang "Wind Beneath My Wings" in a powerful voice that hit most of the notes she was aiming at.

Amid the polite applause as she reclaimed her seat in the

audience, Toni noticed Caitlyn and most of her wedding party walk in. The girls all still looked terrific and she enjoyed a moment of pride in a job well done.

The men looked less terrific—as though they might have indulged in buckets of beer consumed in the sun all afternoon. There was a certain boisterous unsteadiness to them. As they found a couple of tables side by side, the third performer was called up. It was the Tom Jones looka-like and within a minute of beginning "Delilah" he had the audience laughing and clapping and whistling. The guy was clearly a seasoned performer. He combined charm, humor, and a pretty good singing voice and when he was done, the crowd went as wild as a group of cruise ship passengers can.

Toni suspected that what happened next was his fault. There was pushing and shoving and joking from the bridal party and the next thing she knew, Matt the groom and two of his supporters staggered up to the entertainment directors and added their names to the list. "Oh, this should be fun," she muttered.

She turned back to Caitlyn and the girls, wondering why no one had stopped the guys from signing up, when her attention was caught by a man standing outside the club and staring in. She wasn't sure what it was about him that snagged her attention. Maybe it was that he didn't seem to fit. He was in his late thirties, she guessed. And the word *thug* crossed her mind. Something about his expression and the way he held himself suggested suppressed violence.

He was obviously looking for someone and she knew the moment he'd found the person he wanted. He stepped forward and blocked that person's path. The gesture made her think of bullies in dark alleys. To her shock, the person whose path was being blocked was Dr. Madsen.

What on earth? Did the scary guy have a medical emergency? A sick partner or child?

The doctor stopped and they exchanged a few words. There was something oddly familiar about the thug. "Tiffany," she said, leaning close, "do you recognize that man out in the corridor talking to the doctor?"

Her daughter turned. Then turned back. "He looks like a creep. He was on our tender coming back from the Bahamas."

Of course, he'd been on the shore excursion. She watched for another minute and then the thug stalked off. She thought the doctor sagged for a second. He watched the man for a minute and then turned in the other direction and walked away.

It was a short encounter, but it bothered her.

"Why are you interested in him?" her daughter wanted to know.

"I'm not. He just doesn't seem like he fits in here."

"I know how he feels."

WHEN IT WAS Linda's turn, Toni whispered, "Break a leg," and Tiffany said, "You go, Grandma."

They clapped enthusiastically, and she heard another enthusiastic clapper behind her. Turning, she recognized her mama's new friend from bingo. He was alone at a table and looked dazzled by Linda.

Ryan from Brisbane also looked a little dazzled when

Linda arrived on the stage. His gaze dropped to her cleavage as though it couldn't help itself. "What's your name?" he finally managed.

"I'm Linda Plotnik, and I'm from Tennessee, originally."

"Well, Linda, what are you going to sing for us tonight?"

"I'm going to sing a song by my all-time favorite performer, Dolly Parton."

There was a wolf whistle from the bridegroom's table. Linda turned in a flash of blue sparkle and sent a dazzling smile to the table of drunks. "I see I'm not the only fan. This one's for you, honey. It's called 'Nine to Five.'"

As many times as Toni had heard her mama perform that song, she still loved how Linda truly seemed to turn into her idol. She had a strong, true voice and enough natural charm and sex appeal that the entire room fell at her feet.

Everyone was singing along, including Tiffany, for the final verse. When she was done, the applause was deafening.

She leaned close to Tiff. "I might be biased, but I don't think Tom Jones stands a chance."

"She blew him out of the water," Tiffany agreed.

As she made her way back to their table, Linda was stopped several times by people shaking her hand, patting her on the back, and obviously praising her to the skies. Toni imagined her mother's cruise had reached its pinnacle. "Well," she said, when she returned to their table. "That was fun."

"You were amazing," Toni said.

"Nailed it, Grandma."

Her friend from bingo came forward and offered her his congratulations. "I have never heard anything I enjoyed more," he said. He managed not to stare at her bosom while he talked, which Toni thought showed class.

"Why, thank you," Linda said. "Would you care to join us?"

"I'd be honored."

"Girls, this is Roy. And Roy, this is my daughter Toni and my granddaughter Tiffany."

"Honestly, I would have thought you three were sisters," he said, earning the gratitude of two of the three women at the table.

"GRANDMA'S GOT A BOYFRIEND!" Tiffany chanted when they returned to their stateroom.

"I do not," Linda said, but she blushed and giggled.

"You could have had any man in there. You were hot, Grandma."

"We're only ever as old as we decide to be," Linda informed her granddaughter. "And tonight I feel about your age."

"It was so awesome when you won," Tiffany said, still high on the excitement.

"I know. I could not believe it. I was so surprised. Which reminds me, I have a surprise for you both," Linda said, sounding excited. "I bought us all a present."

"A twenty-two-thousand-dollar emerald?" Tiffany asked, opening her eyes wide.

"One day, if I make a fortune, it will be," her grandmother assured her. "In the meantime, look at these." She and Roy had walked back together and it was clear they'd stopped at the picture gallery where all the shore photos were for sale. She pulled out a large envelope with the ship's logo imprinted on it and presented it to Tiffany. She had an identical one for Toni.

"Oh, how exciting," Toni exclaimed. She opened her package and withdrew an eight by ten photo. It was the picture the ship's photographer had taken of the three of them when they'd left on their shore excursion.

"Isn't it good of the three of us?"

"It is." Toni studied it. The three Plotnik/Diamonds looked happy, lightly tanned, and like the family they were. In the background she could see a stream of passengers heading down the dock in the direction of the shopping arcade.

"Thanks, Grandma," Tiffany said, jumping up and giving her a hug. "It's a perfect souvenir."

Toni agreed. She set hers up on the table beside her bed, where she could enjoy it for the rest of the cruise. When she got home, she'd have the photo framed for her living room.

IT HAD BEEN A GOOD NIGHT, and when they woke up in the morning the sun was shining, the skies were blue, and the water sparkled.

"Who's up for Zumba?" Toni asked.

"Go away, crazy woman, and bring back my mother," Tiffany groaned.

Linda said, "You go on. Roy asked me to go to bingo with him again."

"Tiff?"

"Going to the gym."

Toni's main reason for going was to see Alicia. But when she got to Zumba, Alicia wasn't there. Of course, it was probably nothing to worry about, but Alicia had seen something or someone that had scared her so much she'd jumped up and run away. Then, when Toni had seen her later, the woman had tried to convince both of them that she'd been mistaken. No doubt she was, but Toni would feel a lot better to see Alicia at the dance workout. She'd said she never missed a Zumba class and now she hadn't showed.

Never one to sit idly by when something bothered her, she jiggled and flubbed her way through the class. After it was over, she asked in a very loud voice, as though addressing a room full of eager new recruits at a sales convention, "Does anyone know where Alicia is?"

She drew attention, but mostly it was blank stares or headshakes. Finally, one of the women who'd been at coffee the day before said, "She's probably got the Norovirus."

"Oh, no. When did she get sick?"

The woman shrugged. "I heard that twenty-five percent of the passengers are sick."

"Do you know what cabin she's in?"

"No."

"Her last name?"

"Sorry." And the woman headed for the door as though she had a number of places she'd rather be.

Toni knew she'd been pushy, but it was worry driving her. She didn't want to think of Alicia sick with no one fussing over her.

By now, there was a general feeling of uncertainty hanging over the ship. The captain's bulletin the night before had contained detailed instructions about not touching anything and washing hands frequently. Crew members were stationed at the entrance to every restaurant and the buffet making sure that no one got near eating areas without sanitizing their hands. The cheerful group dinners were abandoned as people stuck to their own parties. It wasn't a problem—there were plenty of tables in the half-empty dining room.

Toni was becoming used to navigating the narrow corridors, dodging the carts the stewards used, stepping to the side when anyone was coming the other way, and walking with the slight sway of the moving ship. When a man came out of a stateroom in front of her, she paused so as not to bump into him. He was putting what looked like a wad of cash in his pocket. As he shut the door, he turned toward her and she recognized the doctor.

He nodded briefly and would have passed, but she stopped him. "Dr. Madsen," she greeted him cheerfully. "You treated my mother."

"Yes," he said, as though he remembered her. "Is she feeling better?"

"Much." Before he could move on, she said, "I have a new friend on board. Alicia. I don't know her last name. Is there any way I can find out about her condition? I'd like to take her some magazines or something. Let her know I'm thinking about her."

He shook his head. "Not unless you're family. Wouldn't help you if you were. If she has the Norovirus, she'll be quarantined in her room. Very important to prevent the virus spreading." He shrugged his shoulders and opened his hands wide as if to say, *and you can see how effective that is.*

She wondered if he'd been making a visit to a sick person and, if he was, why he wasn't wearing the protective gear himself.

And where was his doctor's bag?

The door opened again and the same thuggish guy she'd seen the doctor with the night before strode out. He checked the hallway when he saw Toni and the doctor standing there, and for a second she felt he might retreat back into his stateroom and slam the door. Instead, he stepped out. Shut the door behind him and nodded curtly at her and Dr. Madsen before striding off down the corridor.

When he'd turned off toward one of the elevator banks, the doctor murmured, "Excuse me," and strode off in the opposite direction.

She checked out the name card on the outside of his door: A. VLODOVITCH.

There did not seem to be a Mrs. Vlodovitch or any other person sharing the suite.

She didn't know why the doctor was visiting the thug-like man. He certainly didn't look sick.

CHAPTER 9

Any woman can fool a man if she wants to and if he's in love with her.

— AGATHA CHRISTIE

*E*ven though the three of them were having fun, Toni was a teensy bit frustrated. She'd boarded the ship with such high hopes of sharing her passion for Lady Bianca with other passengers, but the Norovirus outbreak was proving to be a worthy adversary. The two women Linda had booked for facials and beauty consultations canceled. And good luck handing out a sample pack. Passengers were paranoid about touching anything handled by another person, even if it contained a mini starter pack of this season's colors.

There was no point even offering makeovers. Nobody wanted a stranger in their cabin and, truth to tell, Toni wasn't crazy about the idea of going to another person's cabin anyway. The virus was spreading faster than juicy gossip.

Toni searched her mom's and her daughter's faces each

morning for any sign of illness. Linda looked about the same, but Tiffany had never looked healthier. The girl was absolutely blooming. She had a feeling her daughter's daily visits to the gym were a big reason for her glow.

"Are you sure the gym is a good idea?" Linda had said this morning. "There are so many people there and they touch and sweat on everything."

"Grandma, think about it. Only healthy people go to the gym. And I sterilize the equipment both before I use it and after. I'm fine."

She certainly looked fine.

Toni wasn't a fool, even though her daughter obviously thought she was. If she and her gym crush were working out, she supposed it was harmless. However, maybe Zumba hadn't worked off as many calories as she'd packed on at the breakfast buffet this morning. Maybe she needed a stint on the elliptical machine.

In the gym.

She changed direction, passing the mysterious A. Vlodovitch's door one more time.

In order to get to the gym, she went up on deck and enjoyed a few minutes in the sunshine on her way. She passed the big pool and the spa pools. A steel band played and a number of the loungers were occupied by reading, dozing, suntanning passengers.

She noticed Caitlyn and her attendants, though she seemed to be one bridesmaid short. They all wore hospital masks and occupied a corner far from other passengers.

"Hi, y'all," Toni called out, ever friendly.

Caitlyn motioned her nearer, then held up a hand when she got within about six feet. What on earth?

"Are you feeling all right?" Caitlyn asked, lifting her mask in order to speak.

"Fine. You?"

Caitlyn glared at the other three, who gazed at her over their masks like three frightened nurses. "Susanne's sick. I told them to stay away from other passengers, but does anyone listen to me? It's only the most important day of my entire life in two days. What if she's not better?"

"I'm sure she'll be better in time," Toni said soothingly.

"She didn't *mean* to get sick," Lauren said, lifting her mask.

"Did I or did I not tell her she couldn't go ashore?"

"She looked fine last night, at karaoke." But Toni had to wonder whether listening to Matt and his drunk buddies destroy a hunk of "Burning Love" had made her ill. The rendition had certainly made Toni queasy.

"Well, now she's in voluntary quarantine in her cabin."

"Who's sharing with her?"

"Nobody. Her fiancé was supposed to come, but at the last minute he backed out."

"Oh, poor thing," Toni said. "So she's stuck paying for a whole cabin by herself?"

The bride seemed very unconcerned. "Her boyfriend's loaded. It's no big deal. But you—I really, really need for you and your mom not to get sick."

"And we will really, really try to stay healthy," she promised.

After that conversation, she decided that a stint in the gym was exactly what she did need. And how she was going to get through the wedding day preparations without decking the bride was going to be an issue. At least Tiffany would be in the gym and she could tell her all about her latest run-in with the bride from hell. Tiffany could always make her laugh.

However, Tiffany wasn't in the fitness center at all.

Toni dropped her subtle act and searched the fitness area thoroughly. Her daughter was not there.

Maybe it wasn't a big deal, but her almost seventeen-year-old daughter was a bit of a late bloomer where boys were concerned. Toni didn't want her finding herself in a situation she didn't have the experience to handle. Toni decided to make a casual tour of the ship until she accidentally bumped into her.

There was a lot of ship. Toni started with the obvious places—the main decks, the pool areas, the lounge chairs stacked side by side like cots in a barracks. No Tiffany.

She moved on to the cafeteria, then the coffee shop, the library, and the Internet café, by this time feeling generally irritated. How hard could it be to find her own daughter on a cruise ship?

Naturally, her mother tiger instincts jumped to the fore and she began to imagine that Fitness Boy had somehow lured her daughter to his stateroom.

Not on my watch.

She finally ran Tiffany and Fitness Boy to ground in the Navigator nightclub, which was a happening place at night, but completely empty at this time of day except for Tiffany and the boy, who sat together in a booth. They hadn't seen her yet and for a heart-stopping moment she watched as her daughter leaned in toward her companion, her face alight with laughter and the glow of a teenager experiencing her first love.

The young man reached up and tucked Tiffany's hair behind one ear, mimicking the gesture her daughter so often made when she was feeling nervous or uncertain. He seemed very sure of himself for his age, which was clearly older than her own daughter's sixteen years.

He was good-looking, smooth, tall, and charming. A very dangerous combination. Toni fell back in time and could imagine that happy young girl to be herself at sixteen and the practiced charmer to be Dwayne.

Tiffany would not appreciate what she was about to do, but motherhood, as she had discovered, was no popularity contest. If she could save her daughter from falling into the same trap that she herself had fallen into at the very same age, she would do it.

She plastered a big fake smile on her face and stepped forward. "Well, hi, y'all," she said. There was no point pretending this was an accidental meeting. They had so clearly chosen this spot in order to be alone.

The charmer turned without a hint of embarrassment or guilt—so like Dwayne—but Tiffany jerked as though she had been shot and blushed a deep, mortified, if-I-had-a-gun-I-would-kill-my-mother-this-second red. "Mom, what are you doing here?" Her voice was low and tense.

"Obviously, honey, I was looking for you." She turned to the charmer and held out her hand. "Hi, I'm Toni Diamond. Tiffany's mother."

The boy rose and extended his own hand, shaking hers. "Pleased to meet you, ma'am. I'm Wade Templeton."

"Why don't you join us for lunch, Wade? It would be real nice to get to know you." She might phrase it as a question, but she used the same *don't mess with me* tone that she used on the Lady Bianca supply team if they were late with an order.

He glanced at her, glanced at Tiffany, and said, "I'd like to, but—" There was an awkward pause and she waited, eyebrows raised, until he finished lamely, "I don't think I can. Not today."

"Well, I'm real sorry to hear that. Maybe another time?"

"Yeah. Sure."

"I came to scoop you for lunch, Tiff. Your grandmother's waiting."

She could feel her daughter fuming with fury and she kept the determined smile on her face until Wade Templeton fumbled a goodbye and made a fast retreat.

"How could you?" Tiffany turned on her the second he was gone. She was so angry her hands were shaking.

"How could I? How could you tell me you're going to the gym when in fact, you're sneaking off with some boy?"

"He's not *some boy*, he's nice and I like him."

"If he's so nice, why won't he join your family for lunch?"

"Because he's here with his own family, except that he actually likes them because they don't go out of their way to humiliate him." Tiffany got up and stomped toward the exit.

"Wait, what about lunch?"

"I'm not hungry." As her daughter stormed out, Toni was left wondering, not for the first time, if she was ever going to get the hang of this mothering thing.

"Did I screw up, Mama?" she asked Linda after she'd run through the entire incident for her mother over lunch at a table for two.

"Honey, you're doing the best you can. It's all any of us can do. But Tiffany's not like you. That girl's got a head on her shoulders that neither you nor I had at her age. I know you're scared she'll make the same mistakes you and I did, but I don't think she's going to. Maybe you should trust her."

Toni rubbed her temples. "It's not her I don't trust. It's that boy. He's too old for her, too practiced. Too damn smooth."

Tiffany had not returned to the stateroom by the time they came back after lunch and Toni suspected it would be some time before they saw her.

On impulse, she pulled out her cell phone and called Luke. She'd pay a fortune in roaming charges from out here, but she didn't care.

"Marciano," he barked in her ear, as he did every time she phoned him.

"Honey, I need you to do me a favor. I need you to do a background check on someone."

"What the hell have you got involved in this time?" He sounded a little irate and she supposed she couldn't blame him. She did have a bad habit of getting into some sticky situations. However, this time she wasn't in one and she was very determined that her daughter wouldn't fall into one either.

"It's not me. It's Tiffany."

"Tiffany?" Luke might not show it often, but he had a soft spot for Tiffany a mile wide. "What's going on? Is she okay?"

"She's fine, but there is this boy she's been hanging around with and I don't like the look of him. He's too smooth, too shiny, too old for her." She thought back on their brief conversation. "And he refused to join us for lunch."

"You want me to do a background check on someone because they refuse to have lunch with you? Honey, if I had to do a background check on every person who didn't want to join you for a meal, I'd be working full time plus putting in some hefty overtime."

"Please, Luke. She's my baby. I'm worried about her."

"What's his name? Age? Address?"

"His name is Wade Templeton. Age approximately nineteen. No idea on the address." She recalled his voice. "But he sounds like he's from the East Coast. Boston, maybe, or New York, but with a private-school accent."

"Not much to go on." He sounded grumpy, which, with Luke, was usually a sign that he was going to do what she asked.

"Thank you, honey. When I get home I will thank you in person."

"Are you trying to seduce a public servant, ma'am?"

"Every chance I get."

He chuckled. "How's life at sea?"

She wrinkled her nose. "It's a little bit stressful. The ship's got a bad outbreak of the Norovirus. About one-quarter of the passengers are in quarantine in their staterooms and the rest are scared to talk to anybody or touch anything."

"Must be hell for a cosmetics salesperson like yourself."

"It is," she said, pleased that he understood her dilemma so well.

"You girls all feeling okay?"

"Yeah, so far, so good."

"I'll get back to you soon as I can on the background check, but I can't do this every time some guy asks your daughter out for a date."

"I know that."

There was a pause, and he said, "Are you in a daycare or something?"

"No. I'm in my stateroom. Why?"

"I swear I can hear someone singing the ABC song."

"Does she sound like Dolly Parton?"

"Strangely, yes."

"That's Mama. We've been getting lessons on how to wash our hands. It's one of the things they do when there's an outbreak. You should hear her rendition of 'Twinkle Twinkle Little Star.'"

He promised to find out what he could about young Wade Templeton and after a few more minutes of chat, they ended the call.

Linda emerged from the bathroom. "Do you have any more of the Lady Bianca aloe and vitamin E hand cream? My hands are getting dry from washing them all the time."

Toni went to her case and dug out a fresh tube. "I guess having dry hands is better than getting sick."

"Is Luke going to do it?" Linda asked, rubbing the cream into her hands.

"I think so."

"If Tiffany finds out, she will have your hide."

"I know. Let's hope she never finds out."

Linda was looking ridiculously happy and Toni realized she'd never even asked her mama how bingo had turned out. "Speaking of my wayward relatives, how was your date this morning?"

"Oh, honey, it wasn't a date." But Linda had a fluttery, excited quality to her that suggested more was going on than putting the right numbers and letters together. "But he has asked me on one."

"Really?"

"Uh-huh. He's from Oklahoma, but he travels a lot on

business. When he gets back to work he wants to take me out for dinner next time he's in Dallas."

"Nice going!" She high-fived her mama.

"There's only one problem."

"Don't tell me—his divorce isn't completely through yet? His marriage is over, but he can't leave because of the kids? His wife doesn't understand him the way you do?"

Linda laughed. They'd both heard every excuse in the book from married men. "No. He's definitely single. But, Toni, he's ten years younger than I am."

"So?"

"So? He told me how old he is and I changed the subject right away. I can't tell him I'm a whole decade older. And now I'm scared he'll find out." She lowered her voice even though they were alone. "I don't want to be a cougar."

"I don't see that it matters. If he likes you and you like him, what's the problem?"

Linda took Toni's hand and led her to the mirror. "You see these lines? The ones running from my nose to the corners of my mouth? They make me look old. That's what."

"But Roy's already seen you. He likes the way you look."

But Linda was too busy putting her palms on her cheeks and pulling the skin upward, making the lines disappear. "See how much better that looks?"

"You aren't seriously thinking of letting Dr. Madsen stick needles in your face, are you?"

"I thought he was a very good doctor. And the woman in the spa assured me he's the best."

Toni suspected the woman in the spa got a commission when she booked special treatments.

Linda suddenly got so insecure that she ran to the salon

and booked herself a medi-spa appointment with Dr. Madsen for the very next day. "I'm just going to have a little filler injected in these awful deep lines running from my nose to my mouth. He says the result is immediate."

Toni didn't think those lines were awful, or deep. She also understood that beauty was personal and so she didn't waste her breath arguing. She said, "If you're sure it's what you want to do."

"I'm sure."

"Okay, then." Maybe she couldn't talk her mother out of the procedure, but she could hint her away, couldn't she? "I did tell you about that woman we saw coming out of there with her upper lip looking like a duck's bill, right?"

"I'm completely confident in Dr. Madsen's abilities."

CHAPTER 10

A woman uses her intelligence to find reasons to support her intuition.

— G.K. CHESTERTON

Whenever there was a ship's announcement—and they were frequent—passengers were alerted that communication from the bridge was imminent by tinkling sounds that reminded Toni of the arrival of Glinda the Good Witch. Sometimes the tinkling sound was the prelude to one of the officers telling them where they were, at how many knots they were traveling, or what the weather forecast was going to be.

Sometimes the announcement was about an upcoming event on board or, like today, was to let them know where they were. "Welcome to Grand Cayman Island!" the enthusiastic voice boomed. "Passengers are invited to join us in the Caribbean dining room, where you may gather to take tenders to the island. We will get you to Grand Cayman as quickly as we can and we do remind all passengers that the final tender back to the ship will be at six p.m."

Tiffany wore a pretty sundress and she'd taken care with her hair and makeup. After the grim specter who had arrived at the stateroom yesterday, and had barely spoken to Toni since, she'd expected to find her daughter decked out in black, her aspect one of abject misery.

Instead, she came forward and looked Toni right in the eye. "Mom," she said, "I am going to be seventeen in a few days. I really need you to start trusting me to make my own decisions." Her words so closely echoed what Linda had advised that Toni would have suspected collusion except that her daughter and Linda hadn't been alone together since yesterday. Tiff had avoided both of them.

She drew a deep breath. She tried to be honest with her daughter, but sometimes it was difficult. "Tiff, I know I embarrassed you yesterday and I'm real sorry about that. I needed to meet that young man and I was really hoping he'd let us get to know him by joining us for a meal."

"And he will when he can. But today, he's invited me to go on a shore excursion with him and I really want to go. Please, Mama?" Then she twinkled in the engaging way that reminded Toni of Dwayne. "I promise not to come back pregnant."

"Tiffany!" Linda said, sounding shocked, but kind of faking it.

Tiff put her hands up like a gunfighter surrendering. "Kidding."

She could rarely resist Tiffany when her daughter turned on the charm. Also, she'd had time to ponder Linda's advice. She only wished Luke had got back to her with the results of the background check, but so far nothing.

She glanced at Linda, not exactly asking for advice, more gauging her expression, but her mother spoke up. "Grand Cayman's a pretty safe island, from everything I've read."

She looked to Tiffany and saw, not herself at that age, but her daughter as she was. Sensible, mature for her age, and beyond the stage where Toni could dictate her every move. She decided to trust her daughter's instincts. "Okay. Have a wonderful time. But you make sure you're back here by six o'clock, when the last tender comes back to the ship."

Her daughter threw her arms around Toni in an impulsive hug. "I will, Mama. Thank you." And then in an outburst that surprised them both, she said, "I love you."

"Wait. Not so fast."

Tiffany paused, her happy face getting ready to transition.

But Toni was still her mother and she had a lot of experience herself with dates who maybe weren't as reliable or as full of integrity as she'd first thought. She had lived life as a single woman a lot longer than her daughter, and she'd developed a few tips of her own. "What are you wearing?"

"Really, Mother? Really? We're going to the beach. What do you think I'm wearing?"

"A bikini. I'm guessing a bikini."

"What? Are you going to forbid me to wear a bikini?"

Linda didn't say anything, but she looked aghast.

"No. I have a little trick you should learn. Probably you'll never need it, but a little extra safety is never a bad thing."

Tiff glared at her, suspicion and a hint of embarrassment in her attitude.

Toni went to the table for her purse. Then turned to

Linda. "Mama, do you have one of those little plastic bags? The ones we put the small moisturizer samples in?"

"Sure do." Linda was as puzzled as Tiffany, but she went to her makeup kit and pulled out a small, resealable plastic bag.

"I also need a safety pin."

That was easy. Linda went to the wardrobe where their clothes were hanging. She always kept a set of safety pins in case of mishaps, like high heels pulling out a hem, for instance.

Tiffany's suspicion had muted to curiosity. Toni pulled out her wallet and retrieved a fifty-dollar bill. She folded it until the bill was tiny, pressed it as flat as it would go, then placed the bill into the tiny bag, squeezed out the air and pressed the seal tight. Linda passed her the safety pin. "I want you to safety-pin this money inside your bikini, somewhere where no one will be able to see it."

"Why?"

"Just in case. Let's say someone shoplifts your bag, or you forget your purse somewhere—" *Or you end up running from your date in nothing but bare feet.* "You can always get a cab back to the ship."

Tiffany took the bag and the pin, but she shook her head too. "You are so psycho."

"Do it for me, so I don't worry."

Tiffany disappeared into the bathroom and returned a couple of minutes later. "Okay? Anything else you want me to do? Implant a GPS in my arm so satellites can track me?"

"Not a bad idea. Glad you thought of it."

Her daughter shook her head. "I am so out of here."

When Tiffany waltzed out of their stateroom to meet

Wade Templeton, Toni collapsed on the bed. Linda walked over and patted her on the shoulder. "It never gets easier. I still worry about you."

"Thanks, Mama. It's kind of nice to know you still worry about me. So? You going ashore? Why should my daughter get to be the only one who has fun?"

"Absolutely! We are going ashore and we are going to have so much fun. That darling young man, Errol, the shopping coordinator, says the gemstones are well priced here. And they're duty-free."

And, like her daughter before her, Toni threw her arms around Linda and said, "I love you, Mama."

Toni was beginning to realize that when you took a cruise ship to the Caribbean, a lot of the ports were very similar. They stepped off the tender and once more lined up for a photo with a trio who could have been extras from *Pirates of the Caribbean*. Once more, they were offered every possible opportunity to buy diamonds, watches, emeralds, loud shirts, cigarettes, alcohol, and an enterprising pharmacy advertised medicines in bulk, including male performance enhancing drugs. There were restaurants and bars, white beaches to lounge on.

There were also tours and activities. Lots and lots of them. The tour operators vied for their business by holding out colorful signs with their main attractions. There were island sightseeing tours, rum tours, snorkeling tours, mountain bike tours. If a passenger wanted to do something, and it was legal, there was probably a tour.

"What do you think? Should we do something?"

"Why not? We've got the whole day."

A man came forward, waving a large sign covered in

photographs. "Ladies, where can I take you today? Stingray City is the most amazing attraction on the island. You will swim with the stingrays. I can take you there, and also there will be some sightseeing and snorkeling our famous reef. All for one amazing price." He wore a short-sleeved white shirt with a logo on the pocket. It said, Royal Cayman Tours. He wore neatly pressed black pants.

"How much is your amazing price?" Linda asked.

He told them and they exchanged glances. "Sounds reasonable. And will you promise to have us back in plenty of time to get back on board *Duchess of the Caribbean*? We have to be back by six o'clock."

"Yes, of course. We work with your cruise ship schedule, naturally."

Three other women and a family of four, parents with teenage kids, stood nearby. As soon as Toni and Linda agreed on the tour, they joined the others and watched as their guide recruited a few more passengers. Then he came toward them, dropped his sign to his side, and said, "Okay. Let's go." They walked outside the secure compound and to a parking lot where a white passenger van sat parked among a throng of other sightseeing vans and buses. The same logo for Royal Cayman Tours was printed on the side of the van.

They got in and soon headed out, bumping over the back roads. The van delivered them to a boat with a British driver who kept them laughing with jokes and stories. The two of them had a wonderful time playing with the wild stingrays who hung out there, knowing the tour boats would feed them.

The water was warm and buoyant, the stingrays like large wet puppies, brushing against their legs and angling for treats. Toni hoped her daughter was having as much fun as she and Linda were. When they returned from the tour, they still had time for some shopping. Linda bought herself a fashion watch and Toni bought her daughter a pair of silver earrings in the shape of dolphins. She'd seen Tiffany staring at a similar pair in the Bahamas, so she felt confident her daughter would like them.

They grabbed the tender back and Toni refused to worry about her daughter. She and Linda headed back to their stateroom to shower and begin getting ready for their evening meal. Maybe only half the passengers would even show up for meals in the dining room, but they still dressed and made themselves up as though everything were fine.

"When is the last tender?" Toni asked Linda, checking her watch. Tiffany should have been back by now.

Linda looked as worried as she felt. "It's twenty after six," she said, glancing at her brand-new watch.

"Probably they're back on deck and talking about what a great time they had."

The Glinda the Good Witch tinkle sounded. "Would passengers Wade Templeton and Tiffany Diamond please report to a crew member. Repeat: Would passengers Wade Templeton and Tiffany Diamond report to a crew member."

Linda and Toni exchanged horrified glances. "They didn't make it back! What could have happened? I never should have let her go with him. I knew better. I'm a terrible, terrible mother and this is a judgment on me."

Linda walked forward and grasped her shoulders. "Would you pull yourself together? You are not a terrible mother. But you need to get out there and figure out what happened to your daughter."

Toni nodded. She had plenty of time to beat herself up later, like in the middle of the night when she couldn't sleep.

"I'll call her right now." Her index finger wasn't quite steady but she managed to push speed dial one. Tiffany's phone rang three times and went to voicemail. Toni left a message for her daughter to call her.

Linda had gone out on the balcony. "There are men standing by with those thick ropes that tie the boat to the dock. Looks like they're waiting for the order to untie."

"I'm going to the bridge. I need to speak to the captain. This ship is not leaving without my daughter."

Toni stopped the first person she could find in a uniform. When she explained her problem, the young man nodded as though he knew all about her daughter and the hold up. "We're holding a last tender but we can't hold it much longer. They can always meet us at the next stop."

"If my daughter is not on the ship when you leave, then you better let me off it. She is sixteen years old and I am not leaving without her."

"Of course. Don't worry. We'll get you back to the island if we need to. And you can all meet us at the next stop."

She called Tiffany's cell phone again, and then she started to pace.

While she was in the middle of pacing, becoming so agitated that she paced faster and faster until she was out of breath, she received a call on her cell phone. "Thank God," she said, thinking it was Tiffany. But when she glanced at her display it was Luke calling.

She fumbled to answer. "Have you heard from Tiffany?"

"What are you talking about? You want me to tell Tiffany about the background check I ran on her boyfriend?"

"No. She's out with him and the ship is about to leave and they aren't back yet. That's why I'm acting crazy. Tell me Wade Templeton is not a deranged serial killer who preys on young girls on cruise ships."

"He's definitely not." The calm voice soothed her a little, making it possible for her to listen. "Wade Templeton is your classic trust fund baby. He's from a rich, entitled family. You know Templeton department stores?"

Toni's eyes widened. "He's one of *those* Templetons?"

"He is. He's traveling with his grandmother."

"His grandmother?" Toni closed her eyes as though a meteor were heading for earth and she wanted to avoid looking at the impact. "Is her name Alicia?"

"Why the hell did you get me to do a background check if you already knew who the kid was?"

"I didn't until now." What were the odds that Alicia's grandson and the boy Tiffany was interested in would be the same person?

"He's probably no worse a reprobate than any other rich kid. But why aren't they back?"

That was the question that Toni also wanted answered. And fast. "I don't know, but she's out there with him now and they haven't come back on board yet. The ship won't wait much longer. I'm going to have to get off and search for them."

"Don't panic," Luke said, in his calm way, obviously hearing the panic in her tone. "They're kids—they probably forgot the time."

"But she promised me." And the unease she'd felt ever since Alicia hadn't shown up for Zumba intensified. "I'm going ashore. I have to find my daughter. I can't leave her on some island in the Caribbean."

"Call me," he said. That was all, but there was a world of support and understanding in those two words.

"Thanks. I will."

There was no way she was going to leave her daughter for one more minute on a Caribbean island with some trust fund charmer. Her cruise bag still contained her ID and her wallet. A change of underwear would have been nice, but she didn't have time to go back to her stateroom. She sprinted to the fourth floor and the gangway.

She was arguing with the security staff, telling them in no uncertain terms that she needed to go back to the island to find her daughter, when she saw the tender heading for their ship, looking like her last, forlorn hope.

CHAPTER 11

After forty a woman has to choose between losing her figure or her face. My advice is to keep your face, and stay sitting down.

— BARBARA CARTLAND

She held her breath as the tender pulled up next to the ship. A smattering of people got off, one by one, agonizingly slowly. She saw a couple arguing. The woman snapped, "How could you not know your watch had stopped?"

"Who made me the timekeeper? Your nagging is killing me."

"Luckily, there's a morgue on board." And she stalked onto the gangway.

Another couple got off, giggling so hard they had to hold each other up. Toni suspected they'd been waylaid at the bar. Two crew members manhandled a heavy-looking box labeled LIQUOR, DUCHESS OF THE CARIBBEAN, and as she headed for the tender, determined to grab a ride back to shore, her daughter emerged, looking strained. Behind her stepped Wade Templeton, his young mouth set in a hard line.

Toni's tension melted and all she could think was *Thank God, she's safe.* "Tiff," she cried, running forward. "I was so worried about you."

Tiffany looked close to tears and Toni had a sudden and unfamiliar attack of tact. Her daughter so clearly didn't want to be treated like a child. She was upset, but safe.

"I'm glad you're back," she said quietly. Then she glanced from one to the other. There was clearly a story there and she decided to play it cool and let Tiffany tell her what was going on when she was ready. When she'd watched Tiff head out earlier, she'd been carrying one of the bright red canvas bags with the Duchess logo that every person on board had been given upon boarding the ship. It was nowhere in sight. Wade Templeton also had no bag. She found it hard to believe he'd headed out on a shore excursion in nothing but a pair of shorts and a navy T-shirt.

As much as every alarm signal in her body was pealing out loud and clear, she turned and headed for the gangway, knowing the two young people were following along with the porters carrying the rest of the supplies that had come back with the last tender.

"Where's your cruise card, miss?" the security officer patrolling the gangway asked when Tiffany arrived.

"I don't have it. It was stolen."

Toni was glad she was there as she was able to show her card, show some extra ID, and prove that her daughter was who she said she was.

Wade Templeton, however, was not someone she could vouch for.

Luckily, she didn't have to.

"My card was stolen as well," he said. She waited for him to call Alicia, but he didn't. He said, "The captain will vouch for me. We know him personally."

Sure enough, Captain DuFresne spoke briefly to Wade on the phone. Wade passed the phone back to the security person, who immediately let the young man through, all but bowing and scraping.

Her tactful mood continued, and she said, "I'll see you back at the cabin, Tiff."

Tiffany wasn't far behind her. When she fell into the cabin she didn't even wait for her mother to begin speaking. She cried out, "It wasn't our fault!"

Keeping her voice calm, which was much easier now that she knew her daughter was safe, she asked, "What happened?"

Tiffany shook her head, looking puzzled and a little scared. "I'm not exactly sure. We got off the boat and we weren't going to take one of those lame excursions with everybody from the cruise ship, so we walked down the road that leads into town. Wade's done it before, and he said that was the best way to find a local guide."

"Did you find a guide?"

"Yes. He seemed perfect. You know how they all line up? And they have signs? And they start calling you over? It's all super confusing. But this guy was cool. He was young, like us, he was clean, nicely dressed, and his sign was really simple. It said *Snorkeling, Secluded beaches, Under twenty-fives*. When we asked about the price, it was really reasonable."

Linda had been sitting quietly in one of the room's club

chairs. She spoke up now. "Under twenty-five? I don't remember seeing a sign like that."

Neither had Toni. "Then what happened?"

"He said he had a van nearby. We gave him the money, we got in the van and we headed for the beach." Tiffany picked at one of her fingernails, a nervous habit she'd nearly grown out of. "First, he drove us to this great little beach and we went snorkeling for a long time. When we got back, he offered us a beer." She glanced up from under her lashes. "I didn't have one."

"How many other under twenty-fives were on this tour?"

Tiffany shook her head. "Only the two of us."

When she thought of all the things that could have happened, Toni's skin went cold. "Did he offer you anything else?"

"I had a Coke from out of the cooler. I ate a big breakfast this morning so I wasn't hungry." She went back to picking at her thumbnail. "Then he said he was going to take us to this really nice sunbathing beach. We got back into the van and we drove for quite a long way. Wade reminded him that we had to be back at the boat before six, and he said, 'Yeah, sure, no problem.'"

An announcement over the loudspeakers interrupted her story. "This is Captain Craig DuFresne speaking to you from the bridge. All our passengers are now back on board and we will soon be underway."

Tiffany waited until his voice died away. "So he drove us to this really pretty deserted beach. We went for a swim and then the guy told us that if we walked around the headland we'd be able to see dolphins playing. They hang out there a lot."

She glanced from one to the other, her face tight. "So we walked away. We left him there, with all our stuff. We were so stupid. We walked around the headland and watched the dolphins and admired the view and then, after maybe an hour, we figured we really needed to get going."

Linda was now sitting on the bed, facing Tiffany, her whole body one line of tension. Toni felt the same.

"So, we walked back and the beach was deserted. Our stuff was gone. The guy was gone. The van was gone." She threw back her head and let out a cry of frustration. "I can't believe we trusted him."

"Every bit of your stuff was gone?" Toni asked.

"Yes! Everything."

"I remember that you had the bag that we got free from the ship, but what was in it?"

"There was hardly anything in mine. A towel, a dry T-shirt, suntan lotion, the book I was reading, my cruise ship card. And my cell phone. Thank goodness it was the cheap one." They'd bought cheap drugstore phones for the trip, all of them agreeing that it wasn't worth the risk of losing their smartphones or accidentally dropping them in the ocean or something. The phone, including plenty of minutes for a seven-day cruise, had cost forty bucks.

"What was in Wade's bag?"

"Mostly the same that was in mine. Except he lost his wallet and his watch. And he had a new iPhone."

"So there you were, at a deserted beach. What did you do?"

"We started to panic. Without cell phones or watches we didn't even know what time it was, but we knew we had driven a long way. We walked up to the road. It was deserted.

So we headed back in what we thought was the direction of the ship. All we had on was our beach shoes so we couldn't even walk very fast. After a while, we got to a small town. It was so small I don't even think you could call it a town. There was a bar with a thatched roof and a scatter of small houses. We went to the bar and asked the bartender how to get to the police station. He laughed at us. He said the closest police station was in George Town and it was a long walk."

Linda spoke up, "Oh, you poor kids."

"It was awful. We told the guy we'd been robbed. He looked at us like he didn't believe us, like we were vagrant kids living on the beach or something. We asked for a taxi, and he said, 'How you gonna pay for it?'"

Linda again, "Oh, that rat. Who leaves two kids stranded?"

Tiffany glanced at her in gratitude. "Wade got kind of haughty and told him that we were traveling on this cruise ship and as soon as we got there we would be able to pay the driver and there would certainly be a reward. The guy just laughed and told us to get out of there. That's when I remembered the fifty-dollar bill that you made me safety-pin inside my bathing suit. I swear, Mom, I thought you were the most overprotective helicopter parent in the world."

"And now?"

"I still think you're the most overprotective helicopter parent in the world." She grinned. "Luckily."

"You know what they say, 'youth is wasted on the young.'"

Tiffany shook her head and did an eye roll at the same time. "If you ask me, wisdom is wasted on the old."

"Okay. Continue with your story."

"I said, 'I can pay for the taxi,' and he said, 'Yeah? Show me your money.' I said, 'Show me your taxi.' There were two other guys sitting in the bar listening to every word. One started laughing and said, 'I like your attitude, girl. You got twenty bucks?' 'Yeah,' I said. 'I do.' He got up and said, 'Okay. I'll drive you.' I said, 'Can you get us back to the ship before it leaves at six?' He shrugged and said he'd do his best."

As she was telling the story, Toni doubted she was even aware that she was mimicking the accents of the various characters in her drama. It was as though she was reliving every moment.

"We followed him to an ancient old beater with no suspension, no seatbelts, no air-conditioning. Before he opened the door he made me show him the money."

"Weren't you scared that he'd steal your money too?" Linda asked.

"No. Not really. It seems weird now, but at the time, I remember trusting him. Anyway, I turned my back on both of them and got the money. I said, 'If you get us to the ship before it leaves, you can have the whole fifty.'" She grinned for a second, her face lightening. "I would not have believed that old beater of a car could go so fast."

"It's like something out of a movie," Linda said, her hands clasped on her breast.

"It felt more like a nightmare at the time. But we made it, barely. I hope you don't mind that I gave that guy the whole fifty bucks."

"Honey, you did exactly the right thing. I am so proud of you."

Tiffany frowned. "I only wish we'd had time to go to the cops. That guy should not be getting away with what he's doing."

Linda said, "I don't even understand why that crook stole

their towels and sunscreen. If they were off walking for an hour, he had plenty of time to pick through their belongings and only take the things that had value. If he got pulled over with our ship's beach bags in his van, he might as well admit to the crime and be done with it."

"I'm not sure theft was the motive here," Toni said, deep in her own thoughts.

"What do you mean?"

"I'm not sure. But I think if the van driver only wanted to steal ready cash out of Wade's wallet, he could've done that while you were snorkeling at the first stop. Why drive you all the way to the end of the island?"

Linda looked puzzled. "If he wasn't after their money, what did he want?"

"It doesn't make sense, but I think somebody didn't want you two to get back to the ship on time."

CHAPTER 12

At every moment of our lives, we all have one foot in a fairy tale and the other in the abyss.

— PAULO COELHO

"What?" both Tiffany and Linda cried at the same instant.

"I don't understand it either," Toni said. She shook her head. "I don't understand it at all." But she was quite determined that she was going to find out exactly what was going on.

"Do you think it was some kind of prank?" Linda asked.

"That's a pretty elaborate prank."

Was someone trying to keep Wade Templeton off the ship? Or had Wade Templeton conveniently paid someone to make sure he and Tiffany were stranded together? He hadn't known that she had fifty dollars. Without that secret stash, they would still be on that island. But why would Wade essentially kidnap her daughter?

The more she puzzled over the strange incidents of the day, the more confused she became.

When she called Luke to let him know that Tiffany was safe, he told her to take better care of her daughter. In one day she'd been accused of being too overprotective to a careless mom. She could not seem to win.

But her baby was safe. Now all she had to worry about was keeping her that way.

THE NEXT MORNING, there was a purposeful rap on their stateroom door. Their steward kept such a good eye on their comings and goings that she rarely knocked when they were in the room, and if she did, it was a tentative, almost apologetic, sound. The person behind the door this morning did not sound apologetic or tentative, but like someone in charge of his or her own destiny.

Toni was wearing a full-length silk kimono patterned in large red poppies. She glanced behind her to find Linda in a black velvet pantsuit, putting the final touches on her makeup. Tiffany had left the stateroom earlier, claiming hairspray poisoning.

When Toni opened the door, she was more than a little surprised to find Wade Templeton on the other side. She didn't know what she thought of young Wade, but she couldn't help but associate him with the anxiety she'd experienced over her daughter's safety yesterday. "Wade," she said. "If you're looking for Tiffany, she's not here."

He was dressed in clothes suitable for one of their smart casual dinner evenings. He wore blue chinos, crisp and freshly ironed, a white shirt, and well-polished black shoes, and his hair was nicely combed. She'd never seen him so well presented. He also seemed a little nervous. He cleared his throat. "I'm not here to see Tiffany. I'd like to talk to you."

He'd obviously dressed to impress her, since previously she'd only ever seen him in workout gear or shorts and T-shirts. And yesterday, nothing but his bathing trunks and a T-shirt.

"Well, you'd better come in."

He stepped in, then paused when he realized Linda was in the cabin. "Would you like to go to the balcony?" Toni asked him. It was the only place in their stateroom they could be private.

"Sure, thanks."

"This is my mother, Linda Plotnik," she said.

"It's nice to meet you," he said.

"Likewise."

She led the way to the balcony, stopping only to pick up her big dark sunglasses, then dragging open the full-length glass doors. Fortunately, both her moisturizer and her foundation were SPF 50, so she wasn't too worried about sunburn as she stepped out into the brilliant sunshine of a Caribbean morning at sea. He stepped out behind her, and she waved him into one of the three deck chairs, settling herself in another.

"I want to apologize for what happened yesterday," he said. Since he hadn't come equipped with sunglasses, he blinked against the glare. His eyes were blue, intense, guileless, but Toni needed more than a direct hit from a pair of gorgeous blue eyes to soften her heart.

"What did happen yesterday?" she asked him.

He appeared confused. "Didn't Tiffany tell you?"

"She told me her version of events. I'd like to hear yours." She'd slept fitfully last night, waking frequently with an ominous feeling pressing down on her. People might scoff at terms like women's intuition and sixth sense, but Toni had learned to listen to her inner warning system.

He shifted in the chair, crossing one knee over the other. "I honestly don't know what happened. We hired what we thought was a tour guide for an under twenty-fives tour, but he stole our stuff and left us stranded on the beach." He leaned forward, all earnest and sincere. "I feel terrible. If Tiffany hadn't had that cash stashed away, I'm not sure what would've happened. I should have taken better care of her."

"Yes," she agreed. "You should have."

"I'm sorry."

She leaned back, thinking. "What made you choose that particular tour operator? There must've been ten or twenty trying get your business." She remembered the throng of eager guides looking to grab business from the crowd of cruise passengers streaming past. They'd held up big signs with color photos of the local sights, which they would take you to for a fee. They called out, vying with one another for the lucrative cruise ship trade. She remembered how quickly she and Linda had chosen their guide. He'd seemed authentic with the logo on his pocket and the crisply ironed slacks. Basically, they had trusted him, believing that shysters and criminals would be unable to get into the secure compound. But how secure was it?

He stared out to sea as though pondering the question. "I don't know. I guess because he wasn't much older than we are. He was dressed like someone I might want to hang out with, not in a stuffy uniform. And the tour was advertised for people under twenty-five, so we knew we wouldn't spend the day with a bunch of old people." He glanced back at her. "No offense."

"None taken. Did his sign have the name of his tour on it?"

"I think it said something like Hang Loose."

"Hang Loose?"

He shrugged. "I thought he was being ironic."

She thought back to the tours she and Linda had seen the day before. "Was he in a uniform of any kind?"

"No. And that's another thing we liked. He looked like a regular guy."

"Did his van have a company logo on it?"

He shifted again, uncomfortable. "No." He glanced up again. "I never thought in a million years that we'd get scammed. I thought those guys had to be licensed to even pitch their tours that close to the ship."

"I guess not." Or else the guy had sneaked in. "Did you get his name?"

"He said his name was Rob. Rod. Something like that."

There was no point in even asking if he'd recognize Rob/Rod again. They'd left the island far behind.

"I'm really sorry. I hope this won't affect you letting me see Tiffany again?"

"I can hardly stop you seeing her. We're all on the same cruise ship." When they got to the end of the cruise, that would be a different story. Wade of the trust-fund Templetons lived in New York. Tiffany of the trailer-park Diamonds lived near Dallas. Once they returned to Fort Lauderdale, she imagined that would spell the end of a shipboard romance that could have ended in tragedy yesterday.

Either he didn't know any more than Tiffany did or he was a very good actor. Instead of pressing him, she moved to another subject that interested her very much. "How is your grandmother?"

He glanced up and away again, back out to sea. "My grandmother?"

"Yes. Alicia Templeton. She and I were getting friendly when she suddenly stopped showing her face. I've been worried about her."

If he was surprised to find she knew his grandmother, he hid it well. "You know there's a Norovirus outbreak on ship? The doctor's been in to see her every day. He's hoping she'll feel better in a day or two."

"Is she well enough for visitors?" Toni had no idea those words were even going to come out of her mouth until she said them. But once she had, she realized that she really wanted to make sure Alicia was all right.

He shook his head. "She's still not well enough to see anyone, but I'll be sure and tell her that you're thinking about her."

"Yes, please do that. And if there's anything I can do, you only have to ask."

"Thanks. I appreciate that."

After Wade left, she replaced Linda at the desk, which they'd turned into a vanity table. Even as she freshened her lipstick, she caught herself frowning into the mirror. She couldn't explain why, but when Wade had told her that his grandmother wasn't well enough to have visitors, she had felt there was something he wasn't telling her.

"That sure is a nice-looking young man," Linda said, emerging from the bathroom with her curling iron in her hand.

"He sure is." Why would Wade Templeton lie about his own grandmother's health? Too many things about that young man were not adding up.

She'd told Linda about the connection between Alicia and Wade. Now she said, "He says his grandmother is too sick to see anyone."

"You sound like you don't believe him."

"I'm curious as to why, if she's got the Norovirus and they're sharing a cabin, he isn't quarantined too."

CHAPTER 13

The more hidden the venom, the more dangerous it is

— MARGUERITE DE VALOIS, (1594)

oni headed to the salon for a mani/pedi. Some women might go to a yoga class when they needed to think. They might meditate or head into nature for a long walk. When she needed to puzzle something out, Toni usually prepared herself a facial mask or ran herself a bath. But with three women sharing the room, she was not going to have five minutes to herself.

So she did the next best thing. She pored over the selection of facials, massages, body wraps, and other beauty treatments on offer, but the only treatment with an appointment available that afternoon was a manicure and pedicure. Toni was never one to turn down a mani/pedi.

When she got to the salon, her nail specialist turned out to be a quiet woman from Serbia. Since Toni had a lot on her mind, she was relieved not to have to chat. Anyone who knew her would have twigged immediately to the fact that she was deeply troubled, but fortunately, Katya didn't know her from any one of the other three thousand passengers on board.

She led Toni to the treatment room, where a black pedicure lounger was already set up. Warm water was running into the basin and as the woman instructed Toni to take off her shoes, relax in the chair, and place her feet in the bubbling water, she picked up a bottle of what looked like bath salts, though there was no label on the brown glass bottle.

"Are you allergic to anything?" the woman asked, holding the bottle poised above the bubbling water.

Toni stared at the bottle, stared at the water, stared at Katya. "What did you say?"

"Are you allergic to anything?" Katya said, more slowly and loudly this time, as though Toni might either be hard of hearing or struggling to understand her accent.

"No. I'm not allergic to anything," she said, and sank back into the chair. She watched as Katya poured some kind of powder into the swirling water, watched as it dissolved so you'd never even know it was there.

As she sank her feet into the whirlpool, her thoughts were spinning just as fast. She barely waited for the Peacock in Paradise color she'd chosen for her nails to dry before finding a quiet spot and calling Luke.

Instead of identifying himself, he said, "Don't tell me. She's got another date."

"No. It's not that." How to tell Luke what she suspected without him thinking she was crazy? She thought about it for a second and realized there was no way. So, she jumped in.

He already thought she was crazy most of the time. "I was having a pedicure and I had an epiphany."

"Really? Don't tell me. You realized that painting colored gunk on your nails is a complete waste of time?"

She rolled her eyes. "No. And this is serious. Luke, can you find out who inherits Alicia Templeton's money if she dies?"

"Why?" Luke wasn't a big time waster and he didn't really like it when she wasted his time, either.

She glanced around to make sure no one could hear her and then lowered her voice anyway. "Because I think she might be being poisoned."

"Toni, you told me yourself she's got the Norovirus. It's a form of gastroenteritis. Goes through populations that live in close quarters, like dorm rooms, seniors' homes, and cruise ships."

"I know that. But what if someone is using the Norovirus as an excuse to poison a rich woman?"

"How would the murderer possibly be able to start a Norovirus epidemic?"

"I had a lot of time to think when I was having my pedicure and manicure. Did you know there's a website that tracks the virus? If a cruise ship has had an outbreak recently, it's much more likely to get it again."

"So you're saying someone wants to kill this woman for her money. How do they get her on an infected ship?"

She nibbled her lip. In the spa, all this had seemed so much more plausible. "Part of it has to be coincidence. She's already booked on the ship. Maybe someone's wanted her out of the way for a while. They discover the ship's had a recent outbreak. They feel there's a reasonable chance there will be another one, so they get on board."

"With poison?"

"Yes." Maybe.

There was a long pause. She only knew he was still on the line because she could hear him breathing. Finally, he said, "Toni, other women go on cruises and they get sunburns, take up with cabin stewards, and buy overpriced jewelry and souvenir rum cake. They don't start making up mysteries."

"Our cabin steward is a woman," she snapped. Also, she always wore sunscreen to prevent wrinkles so she never burned. She and her mom had already bought some pretty jewelry. She was certain they hadn't overpaid, as their lovely on-board shopping expert had told them which stores they could trust. Plus, Linda's VIP card gave them an extra ten percent off their purchases. In her suitcase at that very moment was a round of Tortuga rum cake that she'd intended to give to Luke. Clearly, she'd have to get him a different gift.

"Something's going on, Luke. I feel it in my bones." She'd told him what had happened to Tiffany and Wade when she'd called him last night. Now, she said, "I don't think Wade and Tiffany were random victims of theft. I think they were targeted."

"How does this relate to your poisoning theory?" Luke might scoff at her, but he always listened. Probably because she'd been proven to be right more than a few times.

"I'm not sure."

"Is she married?"

"Getting a divorce. But there's a prenup. He doesn't want a divorce. And if it goes through, he won't get very much. See where I'm going with this? Then there's the grandson who, I'm pretty sure, lied about his grandmother's condition. He said she was too sick to see me."

"Maybe that's the truth."

"Then why isn't *he* quarantined? They're sharing a stateroom. Maybe he's poisoning her. Or he paid someone to do it when he was off the ship. Wouldn't that be convenient? If his dear grandmother died while he was miles away, with my daughter as his alibi, and the whole damn ship as witnesses. Maybe he's in the will for a bundle and needs ready cash for something."

"Like what? He's from a rich family. Why does he need to kill people for money?"

She'd thought all this through as her feet were being exfoliated. "It would have to be for something his family could never know about. Gambling debts. Or a drug problem. I don't know, but I couldn't live with myself if something bad happened to Alicia and I did nothing to stop it."

"You know what they say—poison is a woman's weapon."

Luke didn't promise to look into Alicia's beneficiaries, but he didn't outright say he wouldn't either, so Toni decided to hope for the best.

He said, "Is the husband on board?"

"I don't know. Alicia looked like she'd seen a ghost and freaked out the first time I met her. She'd been talking about her divorce at the time. Could you find out?"

"I'm dealing with a double murder, I have to testify in a drug case that's going south, and now you want me to find out if some rich guy is on a cruise?"

"Please?"

"You must be the only woman who goes in for a manicure and comes out thinking somebody's getting murdered."

"I also came out with very pretty nails," she reminded him.

TONI TOOK A WALK ON DECK. There was a riotous crowd around the pool bar and Romeo, the Filipino bartender, was on duty once more. She watched him make a show out of mixing drinks, surrounded by a crowd of people, all laughing, having fun, nobody taking life too seriously. It was a cruise ship, after all. Everybody was here to have fun, relax, have a drink.

She didn't even need to close her eyes, she remembered so well watching the mysterious salts dissolving in the swirling water. In her imagination, the scene shifted from the salon and spa to this very bar on the day that two men had sent over drinks for herself and Alicia. It would have been so easy for someone to drop something into one of them. They hadn't had the same one, and each woman had been sent one specifically. Alicia was long and cool, while Toni was fruity and punchy. It would have been so easy to distract the joking drinkers sitting around the bar long enough to drop the first dose of poison into Alicia's drink. Alicia had mentioned feeling queasy soon after that and Toni hadn't seen her since.

Luke was quite probably right and she was turning a simple case of Norovirus into a dastardly plot. But Toni could no more ignore someone who might be in trouble than she could prevent herself from looking like a complete fool if she was wrong.

Well, acting like a fool hadn't killed her yet, and *not* acting like a fool might kill Alicia. Really, there was no contest.

But how to get into Alicia's room?

The sight of the blue coverall–clad crew members was becoming so common that Toni always greeted them as she passed as though they were normal staff dressed in normal uniforms. She followed a pair of them discreetly until she found where the clean suits were kept. She waited until they were gone and then darted into the storage room.

"Can I help you?" a startled crew member asked.

She was equally startled—she'd thought the room was empty. However, she'd already discovered that on this ship, maybe on every cruise ship, when a customer made a request, crew members fulfilled it right away. They took customer service to amazing levels. So, she put on her biggest smile.

"Could you get me a bucket of ice? I can't find anyone and I've got two friends waiting and a bottle of champagne that needs to chill."

He glanced around as though not quite sure what to do. She said, "Please, it's for the bride."

She didn't know whether the word *bride* normally made him jump or whether the bridezilla on this cruise had become infamous with all of the staff, but he immediately said, "Yes, of course, madam," and strode so fast toward the kitchen he was practically jogging. It didn't take her more than a second to grab one of the protective coveralls, a hospital mask from one labeled box and a pair of surgical gloves from another, and tuck them into her Duchess Cruise Line carryall.

Part one of her plan was accomplished.

The cruise ship very thoughtfully put every passenger's

name outside the door. Of course, most suites only had two people in them, or in their case, three. There was a schematic of the ship showing everything from the main dining rooms to the individual cabins. It hung in the same spot on every deck of the ship.

She used it to identify which were the biggest cabins. There weren't that many and they were only on two of the decks, and now she knew Alicia's last name, so within less than half an hour, she had identified Alicia's cabin. She knocked, but there was no answer. Was the woman sleeping? In the bathroom? Too sick to answer the door? What if she was weak and in desperate need of help?

The big *what if.*

CHAPTER 14

Love is the master key that opens the gates of happiness, of hatred, of jealousy, and most easily of all, the gate of fear.

— OLIVER WENDELL HOLMES

She returned to her suite, feeling as though sinister forces surrounded the ship like brooding skies before a tropical storm. Though the weather, at least, continued cloudless, balmy, and perfect.

It was inside that things were getting nasty.

She picked up the bundle of papers in their mail slot. The newsletter was padded, as usual, with sign-up sheets for shore excursions, special sales, and reminders of services offered by the ship. Toni flipped through today's offerings and paused.

A photo of a lovely floral arrangement reminded passengers that the on- board florist was available to create an arrangement for every mood or budget.

It was amazing to her that there was an on -board florist.

You could order everything from a dozen red roses to a large and very tasteful table arrangement. She placed the ad with the other papers on the desk. She set to thinking and was still deep in thought when her mother came into the stateroom looking perturbed.

"Mom? Are you done already?" She jumped up and stepped closer to study how her mother's filler had turned out.

But Linda looked exactly the same as she had when she'd left, apart from a discontented frown. The lines that concerned her, running between her nose and mouth, were exactly as deep as they had been this morning at breakfast.

"Dr. Madsen never showed up."

"He missed your appointment?" They were so keen to push all the cosmetic rejuvenation techniques that she was astonished.

"I know. I can't believe it. I finally got my nerve up, and I had my winnings from karaoke, so it was practically going to be free, and the doctor stood me up."

"Didn't somebody call him? Maybe he fell asleep in his stateroom. Maybe he got called away because somebody was sick." Maybe he'd died of old age.

Her mother shook her head, looking disappointed. "They were trying to track him down when I got there. I could hear them. I think they even sent someone to his stateroom to look for him. He's missed all his appointments this morning."

"Maybe it's just as well, Mama. Perhaps this is a sign that you look fine as you are."

"I suppose. But I liked his bedside manner. And besides, even if it's red and puffy for a few days, by the time we get off the ship, no one will ever know that I indulged in a tiny cosmetic procedure. I'll simply look mysteriously younger."

"Did they reschedule?"

"They said they'd call me."

"Well, I'm glad you're here, Mama. I need you to do me a favor."

Linda listened as she outlined her plan, her eyes widening as Toni laid it all out. "Did you tell Luke what you suspect?"

"Yes. I did." Her words came out more clipped than she had intended.

"And did he suggest that you might be plumb crazy?"

"He didn't use the exact words *plumb crazy,* but that was the gist of the conversation."

"You can't seriously suspect that nice young man. He's so respectable. So handsome."

"I have bad news for you. It's not only ugly people who commit crimes."

"But Tiffany likes him."

"I know." That was the worst part. "And I almost let her get trapped alone with him. I'm not convinced he's doing wrong, but I can't shake the feeling that something's wrong with Alicia. Haven't you noticed that people who got hit are starting to show up again to meals?" Looking pale and a little thinner, but they were emerging from their sick beds. Not Alicia.

"I refuse to believe it."

"Because he's so good looking?"

Linda shook her head, so the blond waves cascading down her cheeks trembled. "Because Tiffany's smart about people. And he came here, in person, to apologize to you. I was angry with him, too, for putting our baby in danger, but you have to give him credit for owning his fault and coming to you to admit his fault."

"Unless he was trying to spike our guns."

"What guns?"

She picked up the florist's order form. "It's an expression. It means that maybe he showed up here all apologetic so we'd fall under the spell of his charm. If he's harming his grandmother, the last thing he wants is me nosing around."

"Which is exactly what you are planning to do. Really, Toni. Are you sure this is a good idea?"

To prevent any further argument, she picked up the in-house phone and ordered a tasteful floral arrangement suitable for an invalid. The on -board florist assured her the bouquet would arrive within the hour. In fact, it was only thirty minutes later that there was a discreet knock at the door. Toni held up her hand and the two women waited silently. Sure enough, the door soon opened and a young woman entered holding a large floral arrangement.

"Oh, that is so pretty!" Linda gushed. "I'm so sorry we couldn't hear you knocking, we were out in the patio and you can't hear anything out there with the sound of the ocean."

"That's all right. Where would you like the arrangement?"

"Well, let's see." Linda made a production of trying to decide where she wanted the flowers. "Maybe on the table here? If you could perhaps just move my eyeglasses."

Of course, in order to move Linda's eyeglasses, the girl had to put down her passkey, since she only had two hands. Once again, Toni was thankful that customer service was everything on the ship. Linda began picking things up and helping to make room on the table, getting into the poor girl's way as they tried the flowers here and there.

"Maybe on the other side of the room, on the counter over the fridge? What do you think?" And while she was fluttering, she palmed the passkey and slipped it to Toni. The girl left without ever realizing that she didn't have her passkey with her. Toni knew they didn't have long, so she threw herself into the hooded blue coverall, pulled on the gloves, tied the mask over her face, grabbed the floral arrangement and, with a thumbs-up to Linda, left the suite.

She avoided the elevators, running lightly down two sets of stairs to reach Alicia's stateroom. She passed a couple of people who merely nodded at her or said hello. When she got to Alicia's door, she knocked once more. She could see a light on in the room and as she knocked a second time, the light went out.

For a second she experienced a flashback to the time a much younger Tiffany, an avid reader even then, would read much later than she was supposed to. She'd flip off her light when she heard her mother approaching her bedroom.

Toni used the passkey to enter Alicia's stateroom.

She entered carefully, slowly, not wanting to startle Alicia. She called out softly, "Hello?"

There was no answer.

She walked deeper into the suite, her eyes adjusting to the gloom. The curtains were drawn and without a lamp on it was hard to see anything. She had calculated that Wade would be up on deck somewhere and was pleased to find she was right. Through the plastic lens of her face mask she saw the stateroom was empty but for Alicia, lying in bed.

She'd assumed Alicia's stateroom, like hers, would feature

two single beds and a sitting area. But Alicia's suite was much more luxurious. She lay in splendor in a queen-sized bed and her sitting area was twice the size of Toni's. An open connecting door led to a second bedroom where, no doubt, Wade had his quarters.

Toni placed the flowers on the table. Alicia turned her head. She definitely wasn't sleeping. Her eyes appeared to be open. It was hard to tell with the cheap plastic facemask. Well, it was now or never. She eased it off.

"Alicia?" she said softly. "It's Toni Diamond. I've been so worried about you, I wanted to make sure you were okay."

"Toni?" The woman in the bed shifted, pulling the bedclothes up over her chin. "What are you doing here?" Her words sounded blurry, as though it hurt her to talk.

The good news was, she didn't sound so weak with poison that she was near death. If anything, she sounded edgily polite, no doubt wishing she was in her own home, where her well-trained butler or her private security staff would throw unwanted intruders out.

She reminded herself that making a fool of herself was not life-threatening and immediately tried to explain her irrational behavior.

"I got this idea in my head that you might be really sick. My mother told me I was plumb crazy, but I had to make sure. No one answered when I knocked earlier and I got scared. I am so sorry I bothered you."

There was a moment of complete silence. Then, "You brought me flowers?"

"I did."

An arm, clad in a very expensive nightgown, reached out of the bed and flipped on the bedside light. Alicia sat up.

She saw immediately that Alicia did not have the Norovirus. Her instincts had been right about that. What Alicia had was red, puffy areas around her eyes, her mouth, and her nose.

"My gosh, you never had the virus at all, did you?"

The woman shook her head, then winced. "I hope I can trust you to keep my secrets."

"Of course." Why had it never occurred to her that Dr. Madsen made stateroom calls not only to check on sick patients, but also, in his capacity as the head doctor in the medi-spa, to offer his services in a more private setting? She'd been such a fool.

"Since you're here, why don't you sit down, take off that ridiculous suit, and tell me everything that's going on. I am so bored I am going out of my head."

So, after stripping off the coverall and stuffing it in her tote, Toni pulled one of the extremely comfortable armchairs closer to Alicia's bed.

"You might as well open up the curtains so we can enjoy the view."

Toni did, and in the light streaming in, saw that Alicia's face looked like it was very painful. "You used the Norovirus epidemic to disguise the fact that you're having cosmetic procedures done."

"I took advantage of a convenient situation. I'd already scheduled my treatments. I would simply have said I was under the weather. No one would care. People mostly mind their own business on cruise ships." She didn't precisely come out and say that Toni should have minded hers, but the implication was clear. Then, she added, "I am very happy to see you, though. I get bored watching TV and reading."

"You'd already booked your appointments? So, you've done this before?"

"Oh, goodness, yes. Dr. Madsen and I are old friends. He's been coming almost every day to give me a treatment. I want to step off this ship looking a lot more refreshed and younger than a seven-day cruise would warrant."

"Does it hurt?" She thought of her mother, and of the woman she'd seen holding the ice pack to her lip, tears streaming down her face.

"To tell the truth, I am a terrible baby when it comes to any kind of discomfort. He keeps me stocked with these special tranquilizers. I take a pill when I know he's coming. It doesn't put me out, but it makes me so happy I barely even notice what's going on."

"I can imagine." She could see lines of injection sites, each of them looking painfully swollen, like a series of angry insect bites. The woman's lips were huge and dimpled with red sores, and her whole face looked as though it had been scoured. Dermabrasion, she was certain.

Alicia gave a *What can you do?* shrug. "It's about as pain-free as an attack of angry killer bees, but I like the results. As I get older, and the women my husbands leave me for get younger, I keep trying harder. The happy pills help. And my grandson is a dear. He brings me ice when I need it and he makes sure nobody bothers me."

Toni felt like an unwanted intruder, which she clearly was. She'd all but broken into the woman's suite. "I am so sorry I let my imagination get away from me. Really. I hope you can forgive me." Naturally, she didn't tell Alicia that she'd suspected her own grandson was poisoning her, she simply let her believe she'd been worried that the woman was seri-ously ill.

"Honestly, I'm happy to have another woman to talk to. I love my grandson, but obviously, it's not like talking to a woman." She twinkled at Toni even though she couldn't smile. "Also, it seems he's spending a great deal of time with your daughter."

Apart from being happy that her new friend wasn't being poisoned, Toni was also relieved to find that Wade Templeton was a good grandson, not the murderous, drug-addicted, gambling womanizer her overblown fears had painted him.

"He told me what happened yesterday, when he and Tiffany were almost stranded. He feels terrible about that. I think he's also embarrassed that she's the one who saved the day by having a secret stash of money. Your daughter sounds like a remarkable young woman. I look forward to meeting her when I'm back on my feet." Alicia fussed with the pillow behind her back, making herself more comfort-able. "I hope you won't hold that unfortunate incident against Wade."

Had Alicia believed that Toni had forced her way in here to yell at her for yesterday's incident? She wasn't sure, but she decided to squash any fears Alicia might harbor. "It *was* a very unfortunate incident. But it ended well. The truth is, I'm more worried about their age difference. Tiffany is turning seventeen on Friday. She's young for her age in many ways."

Alicia nodded. "Wade is nineteen but I can assure you he'd never take advantage. I'm biased of course, but I believe my grandson is a true gentleman."

Since a biased grandmother was not the most reliable source, she changed the subject. "My mother was going to have some kind of a filler injected today. But the doctor never showed up."

Alicia said, "That's odd. He's very reliable and he makes a lot more money off his medi-spa treatments than he does dealing with gastroenteritis."

Toni tried to find a diplomatic way to ask her next question and then realized there probably wasn't one. At least, not for her. "Alicia, have you found Dr. Madsen to be proficient at cosmetic injections?"

Alicia started to smile, then uttered a small cry of pain and picked up an ice pack sitting nearby on the bed. She pressed it to her lips. "I know he doesn't look it, but he's very good. Frankly, I often choose my cruises based on whether or not he will be the ship's doctor." She placed the ice bag beside her once more. "I've tried a lot of clinics and doctors. A number of things I like about Dr. Madsen—he's good, he takes his time, he makes stateroom visits, and when I get off the ship no one will even realize that the reason I look so much younger and so refreshed isn't only because I spent some time in the Caribbean."

As she shifted in her chair, Toni noticed something flashing from under Alicia's bed, like glass hit by a shaft of sunlight. She said, "When was the last time you saw Dr. Madsen?"

"Honestly? I take one of those pills before he comes and frankly I lose track of time. I think he was here yesterday." She shook her head. "Wade might know. He sometimes lets the doctor in."

"It's strange that he missed my mother's appointment. They said he'd missed all his appointments today."

Alicia looked up, a worried expression clouding her eyes.

"You think something happened to him?" Panic filled her voice. "You don't think he's got the Norovirus, do you? I have three more treatments booked."

Toni rose, then stepped toward the bed. She didn't answer, but knelt down and reached under the hanging bedspread. At the last second, she paused and reached for one of the tissues in the box beside Alicia's bed.

If the feeling in her stomach right now was a word, that word would be *no,* as in *No. Don't lift up the bottom of the bedspread. Don't pry into things that don't concern you. Don't find out something that in two minutes you're really going to wish you didn't know.*

Of course, Toni didn't listen to the prompting of her inner instincts. She lifted the cover, she reached under, and using the tissue, grasped a pair of familiar-looking eyeglasses. They were men's glasses, with thick black frames and thick lenses. She held them up to the light and confirmed that they were trifocals. That feeling in her gut that had softly said *no* was now rising to a scream. *No!*

She dragged in a deep, steadying breath and with the other hand, the one that wasn't holding the glasses, she lifted the bedspread even higher and peeked underneath.

CHAPTER 15

A physician can sometimes parry the scythe of death, but he has
no power over the sand in the hourglass.

— HESTER LYNCH PIOZZI (LETTER TO
FANNY BURNEY (1781)

When she looked under Alicia's bed, she saw
that the room steward most likely used the
space for storage. A rolled mat of some sort and what looked
like a small step stool were stashed under there. And she saw
that, most likely because Alicia was always in the bed, there
was more dust under there than she would've expected. But
thankfully, there was nothing more sinister staring at her
than a herd of dust bunnies.

She rose to her feet and held out the glasses mutely, not
bothering to voice the obvious question.

Alicia glanced at the glasses, tried to frown, winced with
pain, and then said, "Aren't those Dr. Madsen's glasses? He's
blind as a bat without them."

"Alicia, it's really important that you try to remember what happened the last time he was here. Does he use a different pair of glasses for cosmetic procedures?"

Alicia shook her head. "No."

"Does he take them off for any reason?"

"I don't think so."

"Does he have a second pair?"

"How would I know?" She glanced warily at the glasses wrapped in tissue.

"Did something happen to him while he was in this room? Please, try to remember."

Alicia put both hands to her temples and rubbed them as though she could kindle her memories or clarify the pictures in her head. "I don't know. I don't remember."

"If you think of anything, anything he said, any detail of his last visit, will you let me know?"

"What do you think's going on? Where is he?"

"I don't know." She plucked a couple more tissues from the dispenser and wrapped them loosely around the glasses, then slipped them into her bag.

She sat back down, thinking that if she acted less hysterically, Alicia might calm down and remember something. "What procedure did you have at your last appointment?"

Alicia waved her perfectly manicured fingers under her eye area. "Some filler injected beneath the cheekbones. It plumps the cheeks and helps lift the jowls."

"And he completed the procedure?"

"As far as I know. It's sore enough. You're kind of freaking me out."

Toni forced a smile. "I play amateur detective sometimes." And never on purpose. "I get carried away. He's probably

144

wearing his second pair and wondering where he left these. I'll be happy to get them back to him."

"It's strange he didn't show up for your mom's appointment. He's never, ever not shown up for mine."

But then Alicia was probably his dream patient. He'd likely move heaven and earth to make sure she remained loyal.

"Wait. It was yesterday that he came. I know because I changed the time of our treatment. He was supposed to come at ten in the morning. I told you Wade usually lets him in. I take my pill thirty minutes before he's scheduled to arrive so I'm in my happy place before he gets here."

"Right."

"But yesterday morning, I discovered I was out of happy pills. We couldn't get hold of him, so he came at ten and Wade let him in. I explained that I needed the good drugs, so he gave me a new batch, and apologized for not realizing I'd be out of my pills. Then he rescheduled for two that afternoon."

"But Wade was on Grand Cayman yesterday afternoon. Who opened the door for Dr. Madsen?"

"He's got one of the master key cards so he can let himself in."

It was amazing what people could remember when you let them relax. "You've obviously known him a long time. What does he do in his spare time? Does he gamble?" That might explain why he'd emerged from A. Vlodovitch's suite stuffing what looked like a wad of cash into his pocket. Maybe he was, even now, sleeping off the effects of an all-night poker game.

Alicia shrugged helplessly. "He couldn't go anywhere without his glasses. He's half blind without them."

"Then he must keep a second pair. No way he could go to sea for months at a time without a backup pair." She felt more hopeful that he was out there somewhere, even now, thinking, *Damn, where did I leave my other pair of glasses?*

But that still didn't explain why he seemed to be missing in action. "What about among the crew? Does he have friends below deck? A girlfriend, maybe?"

"He's never struck me as a ladies' man. I know he has a wife in Fort Lauderdale."

"Did he seem different on his last visit? Upset about anything?"

"I'm always so out of it, I wouldn't know." She glanced at the clock. "I'm supposed to have my next injection this afternoon at four o'clock. I was going to take the pill at three-thirty."

Toni shook her head. "Hold off on that pill for now. He doesn't seem to be following his normal schedule today." And Toni would very much like to know why. Also, why his glasses were under Alicia's bed. They weren't broken. It looked to her like one of the earpieces was bent, as though someone had yanked it. Possibly Alicia, under the influence of a combination of pain and narcotics? But then why hadn't the doctor retrieved his spectacles before he left?

More to the point, where was he now?

"Do you mind if I look around a little?"

"No. Of course not. What are you looking for?"

What was she looking for? For something out of the ordinary, a clue as to what had happened in this room and where the doctor was now.

She opened the doors to the balcony and stepped out. From inside the air-conditioned stateroom it was easy to forget sometimes that they were floating in the middle of the Caribbean. The sun glinted off the waves and as far as she could see, there was no sign of land. The balcony contained two lounge chairs—much nicer lounge chairs than the ones on Toni's—with the table set between them.

Alicia followed her and stood looking out the open sliding glass doors, but still standing inside her cabin. She *tsk*ed with annoyance. "I asked the room steward to leave my lounger stretched out and the table set beside it. I like to lie out here in the morning when it's still cool and there's no sun on our veranda. Wade almost never sits out here. He has his own balcony."

"Is your room steward often forgetful?"

Alicia shook her head. "No. Not usually."

What did she think she was going to find on a balcony that was swept regularly, if not by the steward, then by the ocean breezes? She peered at the glass panels of the railing, but there was nothing.

She peered over the edge. Alicia's balcony had complete privacy. You could do anything out here and no one would be able to see. But she looked down on the balconies below. No privacy for them.

Alicia joined her at the rail. "When Wade was younger, he always wanted to toss pieces of ice down on unsuspecting sunbathers below." She smiled at the memory.

Toni gazed out once more. Nothing floated on the surface of the ocean, not even a piece of seaweed. Toni stepped back into the room and Alicia followed, shutting the doors behind her. The atmosphere instantly became both cooler and quieter.

She checked out all the surfaces in the room, but it didn't take long. Nothing seemed out of place or unusual. Finally, she said, "I'm so glad you're not sick."

"Thank you for the visit and for the flowers. They're lovely."

Toni smiled at her. "You're welcome."

As Alicia watched, she carefully picked up her bag. "What are you going to do with those glasses?"

Naturally, she imagined herself taking them to Luke. Which was going to be difficult to do, as she was on a ship in the middle of the ocean and Luke was hundreds of miles away. She stared at Alicia for a second. "I'll take them to the captain, I guess. I don't think anyone's seen the doctor since yesterday. It might be time to search the ship." Before she left, Toni turned back. "Does Dr. Madsen always come alone?"

"Not always. Sometimes he brings a nurse and sometimes he comes by himself. I think it depends on which treatment I'm having, and, probably, how busy they are in the spa and salon."

"What about yesterday? Was he alone?"

Alicia closed her eyes for a second as though trying to remember. She opened them after a moment. "I think there was someone else in the room. It might have been a nurse, but it could have been Wade."

Toni left and headed in the direction of the bridge.

When she passed a crew member she had never seen before, she said, "I think this key belongs to the florist. I saw her drop it."

She returned to where she had borrowed the protective

gear and, seeing no one there, quickly stuffed the suit into a bin already containing other used coveralls. Now the only thing in her possession that didn't belong to her was the doctor's glasses.

~

CAPTAIN DUFRESNE HAD BEEN at the helm of the *Duchess of the Caribbean* for sixteen years, according to the biography she'd read in the ship's newsletter. He was British, trained in Greenwich, and from his picture, he appeared to be in his mid-forties.

Before Toni got to the bridge to see him, she was politely stopped by a clean-cut young Englishman in a white uniform. "Can I help you, madam?"

"Yes. I'd like to see the captain."

A glint of amusement flashed across the young man's eyes. She had a feeling she wasn't the first woman to ask to see the captain. "May I ask what it's about? We no longer offer tours of the bridge, you know, due to security reasons."

"I'm not interested in a tour." It hadn't occurred to her that it would be difficult to see the captain, and she hadn't even rehearsed what she would say when she got there, so here she was confronting this very polite young man who clearly had no intention of letting her near the bridge. A few seconds of silence passed. Only the tiniest movement beneath her feet gave any suggestion that they were at sea.

"Perhaps I could give him a message?" the young officer said at last.

"Yes. I found Dr. Madsen's glasses. I thought perhaps the

captain would know where I could find the doctor so I can return them."

The young guy in uniform suddenly went from looking bored and officious to attentive and keenly interested. "Dr. Madsen? Have you seen him? You know where he is?"

So he *had* disappeared. She shook her head. "No. I haven't seen him. Only his eyeglasses." She didn't bother telling the crew member that Dr. Madsen couldn't see without them, since it must be obvious to anyone who'd ever met the doctor that his vision was poor.

"Where are these glasses?"

If she handed them over, they would no doubt be passed from hand to hand and if there was any trace evidence, it would be lost. She had no idea when she had begun thinking in terms of trace evidence, but she suspected it was the minute she had seen those glasses peeking out from under the bed. "If you don't mind," she said as politely as she could, "I think I should give them to the captain."

He regarded her for a moment, rather the way Luke did when he was trying to decide whether to take her seriously or not. Of course, she had known Luke long enough now that he pretty much always took her seriously. But this young man didn't know her at all. Finally, he said, "Follow me, please," and led her down the long corridor and through a door. He didn't take her to the bridge, but to a small meeting room containing a boardroom table and half a dozen chairs. There was no one there. "Please have a seat, madam, and I'll see if the captain is available."

Toni didn't have very long to wait. Within ten minutes the door opened once more and Captain DuFresne entered the room. She knew he was the captain because he looked exactly like his photograph. The young man she'd previously spoken to followed him inside, as did a third man.

The captain stepped toward her, scrutinizing her much as the younger officer had done. He held out his hand. "I'm Captain DuFresne."

"I'm Toni Diamond. Thanks for seeing me."

"How can I help you, Ms. Diamond?"

She shook his hand, finding the grip firm and strong, exactly the kind of hand that should be at the helm of a large ship. Her initial instinct was that he was capable and resourceful. She nodded slightly and reached carefully into her bag, taking out the eyeglasses using the tissue.

The captain glanced at her and then at the glasses. He didn't attempt to touch them or take them away from her. Instead, he said, "How did these come into your possession, Ms. Diamond?" At another time she'd have found his British accent sexy. She told him briefly how and where she had found the glasses.

"You say they were *under* the bed?"

"Yes. I caught a glint of a lens, but the bulk of the eyewear was under the bed. I recognized them because Dr. Madsen has seen my mother a couple of times. In fact, she had an appointment with him earlier today and he never showed up. I got the feeling that no one has seen him, perhaps since yesterday?"

"Ms. Diamond, I can assure you we are looking diligently for Dr. Madsen. He may have gone ashore yesterday and not returned. I'm sure he'll turn up. He always does. In the meantime, may I suggest that we put those glasses in a plastic bag, which I will keep in my personal safe. When the doctor returns, I will make sure he gets his property back."

She was very happy to pass them over, and even more happy to find that the captain was taking her seriously and further, that he understood without being told that those glasses might well turn out to be evidence of a crime. Of course he was playing down the disappearance, and of course she played along.

When she had seen the glasses bestowed in a plastic bag she stood to leave. The captain spoke. "Ms. Diamond?"

"Yes?"

"I trust we can rely on your discretion in this matter. There is no point in upsetting passengers."

"Of course." Her hand was on the door handle when she turned. "Thank you, Captain."

As she walked away, she played back the conversation. In typical British fashion, the captain had downplayed any drama. He'd even said that the doctor had always returned in the past. Was it true? Had Dr. Madsen disappeared before?

And if so, where did he go?

CHAPTER 16

You can't help getting older, but you don't have to get old.

— GEORGE BURNS

When she arrived in the stateroom, Linda said, "You were gone so long I started to worry about you. How was she?"

"She?" Toni felt momentarily confused, and then realized that Linda had last seen her when she had been worried about Alicia. "Right." She shook her head. "Sorry. Alicia is fine. But the doctor seems to be missing."

"The doctor? Dr. Madsen? You mean the doctor who stood me up?" At first, when she'd returned from the spa, Linda had seemed almost relieved not to have gone through with the procedure. But now that hours had passed, Toni could see that she wished it had been done.

"I'm worried that something might have happened to him."

"Wait. I'm confused. Now it's the doctor we're worried about?"

"Yes. Yes, I think so." She understood that the captain didn't want her speculating and causing trouble among the passengers, but there was no possible way Toni could stop herself from telling her mother about the incidents of the morning.

Linda listened, and when she got to the part about the glasses, her mother's eyes bugged open. "What do you think happened to him?"

"I have no idea."

"Why would his glasses be in Alicia's suite? Did he pull them off for part of the procedure? Does she remember him doing that?"

"No. She takes a heavy tranquilizer when she knows she's having one of those treatments."

"Huh. That's a good idea," Linda said, clearly storing this piece of information for future reference.

"I wish I knew where he was, or how to find him."

"Well, the one good thing to come out of this is that you've stopped thinking Wade is a murderer."

"I didn't exactly say—"

"You implied it. And he's a very nice young man."

"He's good looking, Mama, which does not automatically mean nice."

But her mom had made a good point. Whatever had happened in that suite, Wade had been far away.

"What are you planning to do next?"

Toni said, "Captain DuFresne made it very clear he would like me to stay out of this."

"I didn't ask you what the captain thought you should do. I asked *you* what you're going to do next."

Nobody knew her like her mama. "I'm going to talk to Wade. He's the only one who might have some clue as to what happened. I wish Luke would hurry up and get back to me."

"You must've forgotten to take your phone with you. I think Luke did try to call you."

She had been so busy making sure she had the passkey and the blue coverall that she'd forgotten to take her cell phone with her. She headed straight for her phone, which was still plugged in and charging. Sure enough, Luke had left a message. In typical Luke fashion the message merely said, *Call me.*

She called him immediately and got voicemail. She tapped her fingers against her knee and left a message when she got the tone. Then she grabbed her cruise bag once more. "I can't just sit here. I'm going to find Wade."

As she had suspected he would be, Wade was with her daughter. She found them stretched out side by side in matching lounge chairs, deep in conversation. Her daughter's expression was animated and she gestured with her hands as she spoke. Wade seemed to enjoy listening to her. His gaze was intent on her face.

Toni stepped closer. "Hi, kids," she said.

Tiffany regarded her warily. Wade also regarded her warily, as though he were about to get in trouble. She smiled reassuringly at both of them. "I saw Alicia."

Wade started to rise, but she stopped him. "It's okay, really. I think she was glad to have a visitor. I understand that when you told me she was too sick to see anyone, you were only doing what she asked you to do." She thought carefully about what she wanted to say next, and finally came up with, "Your grandmother thinks Dr. Madsen is very good."

Her daughter was looking at her strangely. She knew that Toni planned to age gracefully for as long as she could.

Wade shrugged, still sitting bolt upright on his lounger. "Yeah, I guess."

"What about you? She says you've been letting the doctor into her stateroom. You think he's doing a good job?"

"I think my grandmother looks fine without all that stuff, but if that's what she wants to do, I guess it's her business." He paused and said, "He seems kind of old. When I got back from the shore excursion yesterday I went to check on her, and they were both asleep."

Toni's eyes opened wide. This was not what she'd expected. "They were both asleep? What, you mean your grandmother and Dr. Madsen?"

Wade crinkled his face in disgust. "Well, not together, obviously. My grandma was asleep in her bed and the doctor was stretched out on the lounger on her balcony, fast asleep."

"This was yesterday? After you and Tiffany almost missed the last tender?"

"Yes."

"Did you talk to him?"

"No. I told you. He was asleep. I didn't want to bother him."

"When did he leave?"

"I don't know. I went to my own room and showered and changed and then I went back out again. I have my own exit so I don't have to bother my grandma. I checked on her again before I went to bed, but the doctor was long gone. The drapes were closed but I opened them and peeked out. I wanted to make sure he wasn't still out there."

"What time was that?"

The handsome face creased in thought. "I don't know. Around eleven, I guess."

Toni didn't like the direction her thoughts were tending. When had she become so ghoulish? But she couldn't shake the notion that when Wade had seen him out on the deck, Dr. Madsen hadn't been sleeping.

He'd been dead.

LUKE'S CALL came as Toni was trying to decide whether she should tell the captain about what Wade had seen. She was certain it was the right thing to do, but she also thought that Luke might have better resources.

"I am so happy to hear your voice," she said.

"What's up?" he asked. "You sound upset."

"I think I need some advice."

"Do you want it before or after I tell you about Alicia's will?"

"After." In all the excitement, she'd forgotten she'd asked him to find out what he could about the will.

"Alicia Templeton is a very wealthy woman. If she should die before she gets divorced, her husband is her main beneficiary. But the grandson's in for a hefty sum as well."

"How hefty?"

When he told her, her eyes bugged out of her head. She had known they were wealthy, but not *this* wealthy. "Wow. So, even if she's talking about divorce, and there's a prenup, so long as she and her husband are still technically married, he'd get a huge inheritance?"

"That's my understanding. Are you still worried that Alicia's being poisoned?"

"I have new worries."

"Tell me it's an everyday worry, like choosing which shore excursion to take at the next stop."

"I'm worried about the doctor."

"The doctor? That quack who treated your mother?"

Naturally, she told him about her visit with Alicia and everything else, right up to her conversation with Wade.

There was a pause. She could imagine him taking it all in, running the story through his various filters and internal police procedural machines before responding. "So, Wade saw this guy sleeping and nobody's seen him since?"

"As far as I know."

"Don't jump to conclusions. Sometimes the simple answer is the correct one. In fact, you'd be amazed how often the simplest answer is the right one."

"What is the simple answer here?"

"The doctor's old. He's just spent who knows how long putting a tiny cosmetic needle into the delicate skin of a very wealthy woman who could end his career in a second if he gets it wrong. That's a pretty stressful afternoon for anyone. So, he finishes injecting, he takes off his glasses, puts them down. He figures he'll just sit outside for a few minutes, rest his eyes, make sure his patient's doing well before he heads out. The boat's rocking him like he's a baby, it's a warm afternoon in the Caribbean, and he falls asleep. He wakes up, maybe he's disoriented. He doesn't want to wake up his patient, so he gets the hell out of there. He doesn't realize he's forgotten his glasses."

"Okay, that's plausible. But where is he now?"

His voice was sharp as a newly honed knife. "That's what the *captain* is going to find out."

"There is no way the crew can do a thorough search of a cruise ship containing three thousand passengers without people being aware the search is going on."

But even though Toni kept her word to the captain and didn't discuss her findings, there were enough people on board who knew that Dr. Madsen hadn't shown up for his appointments that rumor had already begun to spread like wildfire.

"I FEEL like this cruise is doomed!" Toni heard those words from one of the bridal party, crammed, as they so often were, into one of the hot tubs on deck. She had deliberately set her chair close enough to hear their conversation, since she considered the bridal party a barometer of passenger feeling on the ship. If anything, due to the heightened nerves of the bride and the stressful situation, they were a particularly sensitive barometer.

"I hope that doesn't mean my marriage is doomed," Caitlyn said, close to tears, the steam from the hot tub flushing her cheeks. Toni couldn't comment on that, but she suspected some of her friendships with her bridesmaids were very much in danger.

WHILE THEY WERE at breakfast the next morning, there was a reminder announcement about a cooking demonstration in the theater offered by the head chef, followed by an optional tour of the kitchen.

"Is the kitchen tour still on?" Toni asked their waiter.

"Yes, madam. Meeting place is the theater."

"But what about the Norovirus? Is it safe to have passengers in the kitchen? What if some of them are carrying the virus?"

He smiled and leaned closer. "We have several kitchens. The tour will take place in one we rarely use."

"Oh, good."

"What do you think, Toni?" Linda asked. "Should we take the kitchen tour? I wonder if the chef will share his recipe for tiramisu? Not that I'd ever make it. But I love watching cooking shows."

"Sure, why not?" Toni said. "Tiffany?"

"Let's see, do I want to sit with a bunch of old people, inside, watching some old Italian guy tell me how to make a dessert I am never going to eat?" She put her head to one side. "Let me think about it. No."

"Let me guess—you're going to moon over a boy instead."

"What's the point of having a youth if you don't misspend it?" Tiffany asked.

"Fine. Go. Tell Wade I said hi."

She and Linda headed to the theater and found it set up very much like a cooking show on TV. The chef, wearing his big chef's hat and a white apron, stood in front of a kitchen set and cameras filmed him making a prawn pasta dish, broadcasting the performance onto big screens so everyone could see the details. All the chopping had been done, so all the chef had to do was to talk about the recipes in a heavy Italian accent and explain how he mixed the ingredients, and then he cooked the meal in front of them. After healthy applause, he said, "And now we move on to dessert. I will show you how to make tiramisu."

"Oh, be still my heart," Linda said.

He moved along pretty fast, and his words sometimes got lost when he whizzed the ingredients in the blender.

"Are you getting all this?" Linda asked, leaning closer to Toni.

"No. But we can find a recipe on the Internet."

When the demonstration was over, the interested spectators were invited to tour the kitchen. Toni loved going behind the scenes—it didn't really matter where. She liked to see the non-public side of the operation. Linda decided to skip the tour and instead head up on deck.

Toni joined the lineup of foodies and snoops like herself. They shuffled along, through the exit, down a hallway, through a dining room she'd never been in and finally, through a doorway into the vast kitchen.

It was very clear that the kitchen wasn't in use, since there was hardly anybody in it and all the surfaces were bare. Also, she suspected that the working kitchen would be a lot more chaotic. Still, it was interesting to see the huge ovens, acres of stainless countertop, an enormous wine cellar, locked away behind gates, and the massive refrigerators.

At one station, a kitchen helper was chopping cilantro.

There was a flurry of activity in another area where they were baking cookies. It smelled fantastic, and Toni could see ahead of her that yet another attendant was offering each tour guest a freshly baked cookie as they headed back out into the main part of the ship. She thought that was a nice touch and was telling herself that she did not need to eat a cookie simply because it was being offered, when the happy, sweet-smelling atmosphere was torn asunder by a terrible scream.

CHAPTER 17

Someone has to die in order that the rest of us should value life more.

— VIRGINIA WOOLF

It was the kind of scream that makes the hair stand up on the back of your neck. The kind of scream that made Toni wish she'd opted for the seminar offered by the ship's personal shopping director called Time to Talk Watches!

But she wasn't at a shopping seminar. She was here.

She turned in the direction of the scream and saw a kitchen helper backing away from a walk-in fridge, her hand to her mouth. She was muttering hysterically in a language Toni didn't understand.

All the tour guests stood rooted. The bakers in the corner froze. Even the girl handing out the cookies halted in place.

Toni pulled herself out of her stupor and strode toward

the wailing kitchen helper. "It's all right," she said, putting a hand to the woman's shoulder. "What's the matter?"

The woman pointed with a shaking hand toward the gaping door of the fridge.

Toni gulped. She knew she'd go forward even as part of her yelled at her to stop. It was a meat fridge. Carcasses hung from hooks, an entire side was lined with shelves of bacon, and on the floor were boxes. Toni could see where the woman had moved one of the boxes out of the way and in doing so had revealed a tablecloth.

The tablecloth itself wasn't remarkable except for the fact that a man's feet protruded from beneath the bottom end of the fabric. The feet wore shoes. Black shoes with non-stick rubber soles, suitable for walking on a ship's decks day after day.

She recognized the shoes, but, even so, she stepped deeper into the chilled air and gently slid the tablecloth away from the upper part of the body.

Even without his glasses it was easy to identify the dead man, for dead he most certainly was.

Dr. Madsen had injected his last cosmetic filler.

In the few moments she stood there, she searched for any evidence of the cause of death, but she could see nothing. Naturally, she didn't pull the sheet all the way off, so perhaps the cause would be obvious once the police arrived and investigated. All she could do was to make sure the area remained uncontaminated until they were able to get here.

She stepped out to find the scene almost unchanged. She needed to get everybody out of here, preferably without causing panic.

"What's going on?" an older man asked her. He had the look of a former military man, upright of bearing and commanding of presence. He wasn't going to leave here because some woman in heels told him to. She beckoned him over.

When he drew near, she said, "I hope you can help me. We need to get everyone out of here. There's a dead man in the fridge."

He nodded, as though dead people in kitchen appliances were not new in his world. "One of the kitchen staff?"

She shook her head.

He glanced toward the open door but didn't go any closer. "I'll get the passengers out of here, quietly."

"What will you tell them?"

"I think I'll say the woman smelled gas. That will get them out of here pretty quickly."

"Excellent." She nodded, happy to have an unofficial helper. "And when you pass that girl with the cookies, ask her to alert the captain."

He nodded. "You'll remain with the body until the captain arrives?"

"Yes."

"Keep the area free of contamination?"

"Of course."

He narrowed his gaze. "You've done this before?"

She sighed. "Sadly, yes."

"I was a colonel in the army before I retired. Thomas Farmington is my name." He glanced at her with his colonel's eyebrows raised.

"Toni Diamond. I recognize the dead man. He was one of the ship's doctors."

He nodded briefly. "That's bad. I'll return with the captain. I can corroborate your story."

"Thank you."

It wasn't much, but between them, she and her new friend could at least prevent anyone else from disturbing the doctor's rest—or the crime scene.

ONCE THE CAPTAIN arrived and Toni gratefully passed the problem on to him, she returned to the stateroom and showered for so long she was surprised the massive water holding tanks on the ship didn't run dry. Even though she hadn't touched anything except the corner of the tablecloth, being in that fridge with the dead man made her feel contaminated. If she could have scrubbed her lungs after breathing that cold, dead air, she would have.

Her shower was as hot as she could crank the water temperature, but she was still shivering when she stepped out. She dried herself vigorously and then spent time on her hair and her makeup. Maybe her lip liner was wobbly, but the familiar routine calmed her.

And while she applied cosmetics, her mind was clicking through a series of questions. Memories were popping up randomly.

The doctor that first day, helping her mother.

The various times she'd seen him flipped through her memory's screen like a movie montage. She couldn't stop the endless loop.

He was so recognizable, with his glasses and his doctor's bag, he'd been a character as much as a medical professional.

She gasped, staring at herself in the mirror. She knew where the doctor's glasses were. They were in the captain's possession. But where was his bag?

Toni had a mental image of the doctor as he'd been in the cavernous meat fridge. The tablecloth that draped him hugged his body. There was no medical bag–shaped lump. And no bag in the vicinity, she was certain of it.

The last time anyone had seen him, he'd been in Alicia's suite and she couldn't imagine he'd done so without his medical bag. She considered checking with Alicia, but according to her, she was always drugged by the time he got to her suite. Sometime in the past twenty-four hours he'd lost both his bag and his life.

HER MOTHER and Tiffany burst into the suite soon after that. "Toni, I came as soon as I heard," her mother said, rushing up. "Are you okay?"

"The gossip's already out that I found a dead body?"

"What?" her mother shrieked. "I heard you got caught in a gas leak. I was worried about your lungs."

She let out a breath. "No. It wasn't a gas leak in that fridge. It was Dr. Madsen."

"Oh, my God," Linda put a hand to her chest. "Was he…?"

"Dead? Oh, yeah."

"Are you okay, Mom?" Her daughter had probably heard the tremor in her voice.

"I will be."

"What do you need from us?" Tiffany was there. Solid and reliable.

"I don't even know. Distraction, maybe."

But that obviously wasn't going to happen for a while. Linda had to process the news in her own way, which involved talking it through. "He was such a nice man. Remember how he helped me that first day? So kind. Such a gentleman."

"Yes, he was."

"Everyone spoke highly of him. I bet he saved a lot of lives in his time. How tragic that he should lose his, here. Now."

"I know." And personally, Toni would have been a lot happier if he'd ended his life, say, next week, when they were safely back in Texas.

"And he even treated patients on that shore excursion. Plus, he ran the medi-spa. When did he ever get time off? And when I think—"

Toni's mind snapped back to that day in the Bahamas. She interrupted her mother's trip down memory lane. "Mama, do you have those photos you took?"

"What photos, honey?"

"The ones you snapped of the doctor when we saw him in the Bahamas?"

"On my camera, sure."

"Can I see them?" Her voice must have sounded urgent, for her mother looked concerned.

"Do you think maybe you should lie down for a bit? You can't bring him back, you know."

"I know that. There's something I want to check."

"Sure, honey." Linda retrieved her camera and turned it on. Toni flipped back through her photos, then stopped and backed up again.

"Tiffany," she said, "can you fire up your computer? And download these pictures?"

"You deputizing me?" But she was already pulling her laptop out of her backpack.

"I am."

Tiffany loaded the photos and the three of them gathered around the screen as she flipped to the first photograph that showed the doctor. He was striding through the crowd, a man on a mission of mercy. Her mom had been unbelievably snap happy that day and Toni was deeply grateful. "Keep flipping."

Tiffany did. Through photos of them at the beach, of the beach itself, strangers at the beach, the water, the sand, the two of them, then, when she'd asked a stranger to snap their photo, the three of them mugging for the camera.

She had photos of the outdoor displays in the shopping plaza and tons of crowd shots. In some of the later ones, the doctor appeared once more. "Wow. There he is again."

It seemed he was returning from his appointment, presumably heading back to the ship. Even in the still photograph, you got the impression he was walking more slowly on his way back to the Duchess, as though there was no hurry. "Honey, is there any way to put the two photos up on the screen side by side?"

"I can go from one to the other, would that work?"

"I think so."

Tiffany fiddled and up came the first photo, when he was heading away from the ship. Then she flipped to the one of him returning.

Toni nodded. "Do you notice anything odd?"

"Yes," Linda said. "The background on the second photo is blurry. I was having trouble with the focus. Sometimes the background is in better focus than the subject I was shooting, and sometimes it's the other way around. I should read the manual. Except I don't know where it is."

"Not that. Look at the bag."

Tiffany went back, and forward. "Oh, wow."

"Oh, wow, what?" Linda asked. "He took his bag. It's a medical bag. He's a doctor."

"Look again, Mama."

Tiffany flipped from one photo to the other once again. "Do you see that the bag in the later photo is a different shape than in the first one?"

"Really? Let me see again."

Tiffany obliged.

Linda leaned closer to the screen. "Oh, my gosh. You're right. It's so much bigger when he's coming back to the ship. Why would that be?"

"He's bringing something back with him," Toni said. "But what?"

"Drugs," Tiffany said, as though it were incredibly obvious.

"Drugs? You mean illegal ones?"

"Sure. I read about it on the Internet when I was looking for reasons why we shouldn't come. I searched Norwalk.com, crimes committed on cruise ships, the death rate, everything I could think of." She shook her head. "Do you have any idea how many people die every year on cruises?"

"Why didn't you tell me?"

"Well, when I started looking at the places we'd visit, it actually looked pretty cool, so I kept my mouth shut. But there's a lot of smuggling that goes on, especially from the Bahamas."

"What do they smuggle?"

"Heroin, mostly."

"Good Lord. You think the doctor…" Linda couldn't even finish the sentence. "And I was going to let him inject filler into my face." She put her hands to her face as though making certain it hadn't been tampered with when she wasn't looking.

They enlarged the photos and flipped back and forth, but there was no question the bag that came back was bulkier than it had been on the trip out.

"You know what else is strange?" Tiffany said.

"What?"

"That scary-looking guy who was talking to the doctor right before karaoke the other night. He's in the background."

"Really?" Toni had been so focused on the bag she hadn't thought to check out who else was in the vicinity. But Tiff was right. She scrolled through and sure enough, A. Vlodovitch showed up in the background in several of the shots. He wasn't walking beside the doctor, speaking to him, or in any way appearing to be connected. If he'd turned up in only one of the shots, Toni would have put it down to coincidence.

But he didn't.

In the photos where the doctor was heading away from the ship, A. Vlodovitch appeared to be ambling along. He wore baggy shorts, a tropical shirt, a ball cap, big glasses, and carried one of the cruise ship bags. He blended in seamlessly with the other passengers.

When the doctor was returning to the ship, lo and behold, there was A. Vlodovitch again, this time wearing only a white T-shirt and missing the ball cap. Had he removed the shirt because he was warm? Taken the ball cap off to let the breeze blow through his close-shaven hair? Or had he deliberately tried to disguise his appearance?

In the second couple of photos where Linda had accidentally caught the doctor, she'd caught Vlodovitch, too. He strolled behind Dr. Madsen. At first glance he appeared to be part of a group with a woman and her two daughters. Toni suspected he'd tagged along with them to blend in, look like a family.

Toni felt a cold chill waft over her.

"Who is that man?" Linda asked, sounding worried.

"I don't know," Toni answered. "But the nameplate on his stateroom says A. Vlodovitch."

"Did he kill Dr. Madsen?" Tiffany asked.

"I don't know," Toni repeated. "The only thing I do know is that he is on board this cruise ship and if either of you see him, I want you to stay out of his way."

CHAPTER 18

I am not afraid of death, I just don't want to be there when it happens.

— WOODY ALLEN

Toni imagined that Dr. Madsen was stored away in the ship's morgue and that when they got to their next port of call, police would begin investigating. That's what Luke had said would happen when he'd told her in no uncertain terms to stay the hell out of the way. In the meantime, she felt unsettled. She had absolutely no proof that A. Vlodovitch was anything but a fellow passenger who had happened to end up near Dr. Madsen both when he left the cruise ship in the Bahamas and when he re-embarked. Coincidences like that happened all the time.

But all her instincts told her that A. Vlodovitch had not been there by accident.

She recalled the nervous way the doctor had acted when confronted by the Russian. After Tiffany's suggestion that the doctor could be involved in drug smuggling, Toni had done some Internet research of her own. And she hadn't liked what she uncovered. The Russian mob had pretty much cornered the heroin market in Florida and a lot of it came through the Bahamas. Crew members and passengers had been caught with drugs strapped to their legs, smuggled in bags and cases. For all the drugs that were intercepted, many more made it to the mainland.

A doctor with a medical bag? She wondered if he was even required to run the bag through the regular screening machine.

While she was thinking about dead doctors and drug smuggling, she was also preparing the wedding makeup. Very few people knew there was a murder victim on board, so it was business—and pleasure—as usual. Caitlyn was getting married the next day and Toni was a professional. She couldn't let her worries, or her questions, get in the way of work. She was determined to have everything ready ahead of time so that the bride's makeup application would be as stress-free for both of them as possible. She'd also allowed more time than she believed she and Linda would need, because her short acquaintance with Caitlyn told her that something was bound to go wrong.

Her mother was lunching with her new beau, Tiffany was probably having lunch with hers, and recent events had put Toni off her food. Especially anything that might once have been stored in a meat locker.

Instead, she was carrying a stack of towels and facecloths that she'd borrowed from the salon for tomorrow's bridal makeup session.

She was running through everything she had to do for

tomorrow as she hit the elevator button and stood in the hallway waiting. She was the only person there. At this time of day, most of the passengers were eating lunch or lounging in deck chairs. It was rare to find anyone below deck. Hopefully, she'd be finished soon and could spend a little time in a lounger herself.

She was aware that another person was coming toward her and didn't think anything of it until he was beside her. A tad too close. She turned and fought to hold in her gasp of shock.

A. Vlodovitch was standing beside her, looking terrifying. He stared at her from hard, pale blue eyes.

She had no idea what to do. She glanced around, but the surrounding area was deserted. Not even a room steward was in the vicinity. She glanced at the elevator buttons, lit up with the various floors, but what would she do when the doors opened?

She decided that if there were people inside, she'd step in, and if the elevator was empty, she'd pretend she'd forgotten something, turn around and run.

It wasn't much of a plan, but she couldn't think very clearly and any plan seemed better than nothing.

"I would like to talk to you," he said. His voice was surprisingly American, though she swore she heard a hint of Russian in it. And more than a hint of menace.

"My mother told me never to talk to strangers." Really? Had she actually said that? Nerves were making her stupid. She needed to pull herself together.

"Come with me," he said.

"No."

But he grabbed her arm and started pulling.

She had an arm full of towels, high heels on her feet, and she'd barely slept. She was in no mood to be manhandled by a drug dealer.

"I am not going anywhere with you," she said.

Before he could reply, the elevator chimed and she heard the swish of doors opening. Voices told her there were people inside. She was about to turn and bolt when he said, "I wouldn't do that," and lifted his shirt so she could see the gun stuffed into the waistband of his shorts.

"What do you want?" she asked, her lips feeling numb.

"I want to talk to you."

Her gaze darted to the people getting out of the elevator, but they were old and it seemed like someone yelling for help might give them a heart attack. Besides, he had a gun. She didn't think it was a good idea to antagonize a thug carrying a concealed firearm. She swung around. "Fine."

He pushed her forward and not until they'd gone a ways down the starboard corridor did she realize this was where his stateroom was. She stopped moving. "I'm not going into your stateroom with you."

"Shut up." He put a hand in the middle of her back and pressed her forward.

She didn't think he had the gun out and pointing at her, but she experienced an itching sensation in her mid-back as though there were a bull's-eye painted on it.

He opened the door with his key card and held it for her. One last glance up and down the long corridor revealed a couple of stewards way down at the end. Even as she contemplated screaming as loudly as she could, he shoved her inside, causing her to stumble and drop the towels on the floor in the middle of his stateroom.

The stateroom was a smaller version of hers. No seating area or pull-out bed, just a double bed, small desk, the mini-bar, TV, and one chair. He also had a balcony, though the doors were shut. There was nowhere to run. If she screamed, who would hear her?

His place was a lot neater than hers. With three of them sharing, the surfaces had become cluttered. A. Vlodovitch's stateroom was bare. Not so much as a pair of swimming trunks or a towel gave evidence that anyone was actually staying here. For some reason, the super tidiness added to her sense of dread. "What do you want?" she asked. She tried to sound tough but she didn't believe she'd pulled it off.

"I hear you found the doctor."

"You heard wrong." How had her own mother heard the rumor about the gas leak while this scary man seemed to know enough of the real story to drag her in here at gunpoint?

He pulled the gun out of his pants and laid it, very deliberately, on the top of the mini-bar, where a small tray table held a wine bucket, two water glasses, and the TV remote. When he laid the gun down, she heard a clicking sound as it hit the table. "Do not mess with me," he said.

"I'm telling the truth. I didn't find him. I was there when someone else did."

His hard gaze narrowed on her face. "Who found him?"

"A kitchen helper. She started screaming and backed away. That's when I went forward."

"And what, exactly, did you find?"

She shuddered in spite of herself. He'd made the picture flash in front of her again—the shoes sticking out from under the tablecloth and the sad, blank face that seemed so vulnerable without his glasses. "You know what I saw."

"Tell me anyway, Ms. Diamond."

Oh, no. He even knew her name. He probably also knew that she was traveling with the two people she cared about most in the world.

She sucked in a breath. "I saw Dr. Madsen. He was dead."

"How long had he been dead?"

"How should I know?" Just in time, she stopped herself from blurting, "Didn't you put him there?"

He tapped his fingertips on the tabletop, too near the firearm for her to think the gesture was absent-minded. He knew exactly what he was doing. He was terrifying her.

He was a bully, and she didn't respond well to bullies.

"What was he wearing?"

"What was he wearing? Are you his fashion consultant?"

"Do not mess with me."

"Oh, for heaven's sake. He was wearing a tablecloth."

She had a second's satisfaction when he clearly had no idea how to respond. "A tablecloth."

"Well, the tablecloth was covering him. It was the same ones we have in the dining rooms every night. I saw his shoes. And," she gulped, "his face."

"Where was his medical bag?"

Her gaze jerked to his. She'd figured out, of course, that this man, the doctor, and whatever was in the black bag were connected, but it hadn't occurred to her that he wouldn't know where the bag was.

"I don't know."

He tapped his fingers again, the tips brushing the handle of the gun. "You know what was in it?"

She licked dry lips. "No."

"I don't know what you think you know, or what game you're playing, but it would really be in your best interest to tell me where the doctor's medical bag is."

"Why would I know?" All of a sudden it seemed ridiculous, her standing here getting bullied by some thug, with a snowdrift of dropped towels at her feet.

"Because you seemed a little too cozy with the good doctor for my liking."

That was so unfair her jaw dropped. "He treated my mother. When you saw me talking to him outside your suite, I was thanking him."

"And you were the one who found him. What a coincidence."

"No," she repeated. "I did not find him. A kitchen helper found him."

They seemed to be at an impasse. And she'd had enough. She'd had no sleep, a man had been murdered on her cruise ship, which had also been struck with the Norovirus. She had little time to prepare for the wedding tomorrow, and now she had to go back to the salon and get a stack of fresh towels. Assuming she lived that long.

She glared at the thug. "Are you going to shoot me or what?"

She thought a flash of humor crossed the polar vortex of his gaze. "Haven't decided yet."

"Well, my boyfriend is a cop, so I can assure you that if anything happens to me or my family, he will not rest until he hunts you down."

The thug did not look terrified. He said, "Your boyfriend's a cop?" like he didn't believe her. "What's his name?"

She sent him a withering look. "You know cops? They're your personal friends?"

"I know all kinds of people." Crooked cops, probably. Well, Luke was many things, but he would never, ever break the law he was sworn to uphold.

"Luke Marciano. Dallas PD."

He let out a breath. "If I let you walk out that door, what are you going to do?"

"Run to my stateroom and throw up, probably." She wasn't kidding either. This whole thing was making her feel sick. Then she'd call Luke, or maybe she'd run straight to the captain and tell him she'd been assaulted, held at gunpoint, and confined against her will.

A. Vlodovitch must know that's what she'd do.

But what he did next surprised her. He picked up a cell phone, put a call in to the Dallas PD, and then he asked for Luke Marciano. He listened for a second, then hung up.

"Your boyfriend's a detective."

"I know."

"He like your smart mouth?"

She raised her eyebrows at him.

He seemed to be debating something, then he picked up his gun and headed for a black case in the corner. She contemplated making a run for it but she'd be dead before she got past the towels.

He returned, not with some instrument of torture as she'd feared, but with a leather folder the size of his hand and flipped it open. She glanced at the shield and back to his face. "You're kidding me."

"I'm DEA."

"Is your name really A. Vlodovitch?"

"Alexei. Yeah, it really is my name."

"So you didn't kill Dr. Madsen?"

"No. And I'd really like to find out who did."

"Are there drugs in that bag?"

He nodded.

"I don't understand what's going on."

"Madsen was smuggling. We knew it and we figured we could turn him and bust the whole ring. I came on this cruise and made the doctor a proposition. He could be arrested publicly and go straight to jail to await trial, or he could deliver the money, get the drugs, and then deliver them to his contacts in Florida. The same as usual. Except that he'd be working for us, and we'd bust the ring. In return, he'd get a reduced sentence. He took the deal."

"Is that why you followed him on our shore excursion to the Bahamas?"

He glanced at her with something like respect. "Yes. I've been sticking with him the entire trip. When people turn once, they can turn again. We were waiting until he made the final drop in Fort Lauderdale, but that's not going to happen now."

"So you didn't kill him?"

"No! I was trying to save his useless carcass."

"Then who did?"

"I was hoping you might have the answer to that, Ms. Diamond."

She thought hard. Not that she'd looked very carefully, but there hadn't been a big bloom of blood on that tablecloth, no knife hilts sticking out, and he hadn't been strangled. "How did he die?"

"We can't confirm anything without an autopsy, but one

of the other doctors examined him. He found a needle puncture wound and certain aspects of the body that suggest he was shot full of Botox."

"Killed with his own medicine."

"Looks like it."

"But, if the drug ring found out he'd betrayed them, then whoever they sent to kill him must be on board still. And the drugs must be, too."

"Most likely."

She sighed and bent to retrieve her pile of towels. "And I thought cruises were supposed to be relaxing."

CHAPTER 19

Beauty without expression is boring.

— RALPH WALDO EMERSON

*A*fter she left Alexei Vlodovitch, she headed straight for her stateroom, relieved to find it empty and she called Luke and told him about her run in with the thug who turned out to be DEA.

"So, if the doctor was murdered on board—"

"Then chances are, the murderer is still on that ship."

So not what she wanted to hear. "But wouldn't they jump overboard in SCUBA gear or something? Why wait around when they could get caught?"

"They'd need a killer who was also a diver, a boat nearby, and they risk losing the drugs. I think they'll take a chance that with so many passengers and crew, they can slip the stuff past. They'd find someone who seems harmless. That's why Vlodovitch suspected you."

"You think I'm harmless?"

"No. But I know you. He doesn't."

"I can't stand thinking there's a killer on board."

"Now you listen to me, and you listen carefully. You keep your head down and your nose clean. There are cops being paid way too little money, but it is their job to find out what happened to the doctor. What is your job?"

Even though it was a rhetorical question, she answered anyway. "My job is to make sure my daughter is safe, my mother is safe, and I am safe."

"Exactly. And what puts you and your daughter and your mother in danger?"

"Luke—"

"You snooping. That's what puts everybody in danger. Promise me, Toni, you'll stay out of this or I will have no choice but to fly down there and haul you off that ship."

She had to smile. Sometimes she liked the tough guy in him. "Okay."

She wouldn't *actively* snoop, but she'd definitely be keeping her eyes and ears open.

But it was going to be difficult to act like a woman on vacation and not to scrutinize every person on board and wonder if they were a drug ring killer masquerading as a passenger. Or a crew member.

She was checking that she had everything for the bridal party when her daughter came in. "Hi, Mom. I'm getting my bathing suit, then heading up on deck. Wade's grandmother told him to tell me to tell you that she'll probably come down for dinner tonight."

"I feel so foolish," Toni said, "thinking that poor woman was being poisoned. And when I think of the way I barged in there, dressed like a crew member, it's amazing she spoke to me at all."

"You were only making sure she was okay," Tiffany said soothingly.

"I made a fool of myself. You should have seen me in that coverall. And it turned out it was the doctor who was in danger, not Alicia."

"Well, nobody ever accused you of being too subtle. But you were right. She *was* being poisoned."

"What?"

Tiffany put her eyebrows up. "Bovine toxin? *Toxin* being another word for *poison?* That's how that stuff works, you know—the poison paralyzes your muscles so they can't do the things that cause wrinkles. Like smile or frown."

Toni stood there for a second, stunned at her own stupidity. Suddenly, she grabbed her bag. "Where's Wade?" she asked Tiff.

Her daughter blinked at the sudden change of subject. "I think he's getting changed too."

"Get hold of him," she snapped. "Tell him not to leave his grandmother alone. Not for a second."

She ran for the door.

"Where are you going?" Tiffany yelled.

"To Alicia's stateroom." She only hoped she wasn't too late.

"Are you deranged? You can't go barging into that poor woman's stateroom again. They'll send the cops to get you, for sure."

"There's no time to explain," she said. "Please. Just do it."

"But—" Toni didn't stay to hear the rest. Her sense of urgency was too great.

She sprinted down to Alicia's suite.

As she did, she realized that things weren't adding up. A drug ring killer who'd shot the doctor full of a cosmetic drug? Luke's words hovered in her mind. *Poison is a woman's weapon.*

When she got to Alicia's suite, she banged on the door, yelling, "Alicia, it's me, Toni."

No one answered. She kept banging until finally the door opened and Wade stood before her, looking bewildered, his phone in his hand. "Ms. Diamond. I've got Tiff on the phone."

"Wade, where's your grandmother?"

He sent her a puzzled look. "She went out."

"Where? When?"

"I don't know. Maybe ten minutes ago? Twenty? She got a phone call on the room phone. She stood up suddenly and said she was going out."

"No. She muttered something, I think it was something about David, her husband, and then she left."

"I've been so blind." She turned to leave, hoping she wasn't too late.

"Wait," he said, "What's going on? Is she okay?"

She turned, said, "Here's what I need you to do," and hurled rapid instructions at him. Then she ran.

She retraced the path she'd taken to the bride's stateroom the day before yesterday, racing up the stairs because the elevators were too slow. Praying she was wrong even as she grew more certain that she was right.

She pounded down the corridor, past Caitlyn's suite. She knew the bridal party was all grouped together, but not exactly who was in which suite. She squinted at name cards until she found the one she wanted. Then she knocked on the door.

Nothing.

She banged, harder this time.

Nothing.

"Susanne?" she yelled.

Nothing.

She banged again. "Sondra?"

She waited.

The door opened. For the second time in one day Toni found herself being threatened with a firearm, but instinct told her that this time she was in a lot more danger than the first time.

The woman who had called herself Susanne held a nasty-looking gun. It matched the nasty expression on her face. Toni wasn't any kind of expert, but this one looked smaller and fancier than the firearm Alexei had threatened her with earlier. "You'd better come in."

"You look pretty good for someone who's sick with the Norovirus," Toni said.

The woman smiled thinly. "I believe you know Alicia."

Alicia Templeton sat in the single armchair, her face frozen in fear and shock. She stared at Toni. "How did you know?"

"How did I know that Susanne here is really Sondra? The woman your husband is having an affair with?"

"The woman he's going to marry," Sondra corrected her.

"Do you really think he's going to marry the woman who attempted to murder his wife?"

"He'll never know a thing about it." She seemed assured, completely in control. Even now, knowing that she was a crazed murderer, Toni saw nothing in her face that would suggest it. Even her eyes looked sane. If anything, she was amused. "Of course he's going to marry me. He'll have me and Alicia's money. It's not like she'll be needing it. Sorry, Toni, but you're going to have to go too. Loose ends, you know. If you'd kept your nose out of other people's business, you would have lived longer."

Not the first time she'd been warned about her nosy tendencies, but this was not the time to dwell on her personal shortcomings.

"You killed the doctor." She made it a statement, not a question, but Sondra answered anyway.

"I didn't mean to. I planned the timing so carefully. Made sure Wade was out of the way and that the doctor would be finished trying to make the old hag look young again and she'd be tripping on drugs. I'd stick her full of Botox and she'd never know what hit her." She scowled. "Of course, the doctor would get blamed for killing her. He'd lose his license, get sued, but it was really time he retired anyway."

"It's not a bizarre coincidence that you and Alicia are on the same cruise, is it?"

While she talked, she glanced rapidly around the suite. To her horror, she saw a syringe full of liquid sitting on a folded white towel on top of the desk. Surgical gloves sat beside it.

"Of course not. I've planned this for months."

Alicia spoke, her voice almost toneless. "Did David know?"

"No. And he'll never know. It was a perfect plan." She glared at Alicia. "And it would be done by now if you weren't so stupid. Why did you change your appointment?" She turned the gun on Alicia, who said, "I ran out of my pills."

"Moron. I figured she'd be tripping on her happy drugs, Wade on shore and the doctor long gone."

"I knew that wasn't a simple theft when Wade and Tiffany were left stranded, all their things stolen."

"Pretty smart, aren't you? I set that up before we left Fort Lauderdale. Flew out for a day and found myself a kid who didn't mind pulling off a simple theft and getting paid well to do it. I gave him half of the money up front and he got the other half when he left those two way up the island. I had him post photos to a certain Internet site, then wired the rest of the money. They were supposed to be gone all night, but it didn't matter, so long as Wade wasn't around when I paid a visit to his grandmother."

"You went to a lot of trouble."

"Of course I did. This is my future we're talking about. It was all going perfectly. Even the Norovirus helped make it easy for me. I wore a stolen blue coverall and carried a tray of food so anyone would think I was a crew member taking sustenance to a sick person. I was about to inject her when the doctor walked in on me. He pulled me off, tried to fight me." She shrugged. "I had no choice. Had to stick him instead."

Toni could see it happening as though she were watching a movie. "You thought, no big deal, you'd just throw him overboard."

Sondra's eyebrows rose. "How did you know that?"

Toni wasn't particularly trying to show off to a murderer. She was stalling for time, hoping Wade had understood her rapid-fire instructions. That he'd believed her. Hopefully Tiff had convinced him that her mom wasn't crazy.

Everything came down to Wade and Tiffany now.

"You dragged him outside. At some point, his glasses fell off, but I'm guessing you never noticed. He was heavy and you were struggling. You got him out onto the balcony, figured you'd shut the drapes and leave him out there on a lounger until it was dark and the ship had set sail again, then you'd sneak back in and throw him overboard. But when you got out there, you realized you couldn't do it, could you?"

"Darn balconies."

"I don't understand," Alicia said. She might be terrified, but she also must know that the longer they could keep Sondra talking, the longer they'd both stay alive.

Toni answered, "Remember how you told me Wade used to beg to throw ice cubes off your balcony so he could hit the sunbathers below? If you look down off your balcony, there are others below that extend further out. If you dropped something from yours—like a dead body, for instance—it would land on the balcony below."

"Oh, I see."

"So, Sondra had to come up with something else. And you did, didn't you?"

"I still had the suit. I also had the doctor's passkey. Nobody was around in the medi-spa, so I borrowed a stretcher on wheels. Hauled him out and down to the kitchen. I figured he'd last in the meat fridge. If it hadn't been for you, they wouldn't have found him until we were back in port and all of us off the ship."

"I can't believe this," Alicia said. She put shaky hands to her temples. "You're saying the doctor's dead because of me?"

"He's dead because of Sondra," Toni said tightly. "She murdered him."

"And now I'm going to murder you two. You're pissing me off. I can't stand the pair of you—entitled bitches. Anything you want to say before you're fish food?"

Toni glanced toward the sliding doors and Sondra said, "Oh, yeah. My balcony offers an unobstructed trip. But you won't care. You'll be dead."

The woman rose and retrieved the syringe she'd already prepared. It seemed very full to Toni. She knew that cosmetically, the toxin was administered in parts per billion. She suspected a full syringe of the stuff would easily kill both her and Alicia.

She kept her ears tuned, hoping for some commotion outside. But she couldn't hear anything over the sound of the air conditioning.

"You don't seriously think you're going to get away with this?"

"Ah, yeah. I do. I've been planning it for months. Even sucked up to that bitch so she'd invite me to be a bridesmaid. I needed to get on this cruise, and I needed cover."

"But how did you know I'd be on this cruise?" Alicia asked, sounding stunned.

"Oh, please. You think David doesn't tell me everything? I knew he was planning the cruise with you. He wanted the two of you back together, mostly because he has very expensive tastes and I have very expensive tastes and his income does not nearly cover them. I heard this bitch who goes to my gym drone on about her love life to her friend until they made me sick. But when she said she'd decided to get married at sea, I started thinking. Caitlyn does not keep friends. Plus, it was obvious that she only wanted gorgeous women who weren't blond to be her bridesmaids. I started acting friendly at the gym. Next thing, we're besties." She made a gagging motion, putting two fingers of the hand not holding the gun into her mouth.

"But how could you possibly know she'd choose this cruise? The one Alicia was on?"

Sondra flicked her hair over her shoulder. As much as she wanted them dead, Toni could see that she was dying to tell someone how smart she'd been because she'd sure as hell never be able to tell anyone in the future. "Please, you think Caitlyn chose this cruise?"

Toni replayed the chatter from the afternoon she and her mama had given the bridesmaids free makeup application lessons. "She said you got her a deal she couldn't pass up through your travel agent."

"I subsidized all the tickets for the wedding party. Told the travel agent it was a secret wedding gift and forbade her to tell Caitlyn or the other bridesmaids. She didn't care. She got the business."

"That must have cost a fortune."

She shrugged. "It was an investment."

The ship rocked gently. She recalled an earlier announcement from the bridge that there was a storm in the forecast. An image of her and Alicia tossed into stormy seas flashed before her but she forced it back.

"But she still didn't ask you to be her bridesmaid, did she?"

Sondra's scowl rivaled Caitlyn's pout, she'd simply been better at hiding it. "No. She didn't. I went to all that trouble and she said how she'd love to have me but she and Matt had agreed on four attendants each."

"So one of the bridesmaids suddenly fell ill. The one who also went to your gym."

Sondra shrugged. "What can I say? You should always keep an eye on your water bottle at the gym. Otherwise, it might get tampered with."

"You made a girl sick so you could—I can't believe what I'm hearing." Alicia was trembling and Toni thought it was from anger as much as stress.

Sondra glanced at her watch as though she had a schedule to keep and was falling behind.

Toni asked, "Who's Susanne?"

"My sister. My married sister. I borrowed her passport when I was at her place. No way anyone would connect David's girlfriend with a married CPA."

"How did you figure out Susanne was really Sondra?" Alicia asked Toni.

"I didn't until today. But a lot of little things fell into place." She turned to Sondra. "Like when Caitlyn called your name and you didn't answer at first. As though it wasn't a name you usually answer to. And Alicia had mentioned that David bought you an expensive piece of jewelry. When you were showing off your engagement ring, it was obviously new. Also, my mother and I had been looking at a lot of jewelry that day. I remember thinking your ring looked more like a dinner ring than an engagement ring." She took a step closer. Maybe if she could get Sondra angry she'd lose her focus and Toni could make a grab for the gun. "David never proposed. Or planned to."

That made Sondra mad, as she'd hoped, but her aim was

steady. She held up her left hand so the large emerald and diamond ring flashed. "Oh, he'll marry me, all right. But you won't be around to see it."

That flash of green and diamond had Alicia's eyes widening. "That's the jewelry I thought was for my birthday present?"

Her pain and anger seemed to amuse Sondra with an *O*. "Here's a present from me to take to a watery grave with you." She reached over, still keeping the gun trained on Toni, and opened the bottom drawer of the desk. With her free hand she pulled out a very familiar looking doctor's bag. "I thought I might find some drugs in here that would come in handy. And I found drugs, all right. Packages of heroin. I'll plant this in Wade's stuff where Security is bound to find it. Even if he's tempted to make a stink about what happened to you, he'll be too busy fighting drug-smuggling charges. That boy will spend his best years in jail. In fact, if I can figure out a way to do it, I'll pin your murder on him now that the doctor can't be blamed. That would be fun."

Alicia was pale, her face set. Fear had been replaced by anger. "You leave my grandson out of this."

"Yeah. Probably not."

CHAPTER 20

I intend to live forever, or die trying

— GROUCHO MARX

"No!" And with a muffled scream, Alicia abandoned caution and ran at Sondra.

Sondra transferred the gun to her left hand and grabbed the hypodermic needle.

"Alicia, stop," Toni yelled.

But Sondra had finished talking. She wanted to kill somebody. She advanced on Alicia with a stabbing motion, like Norman Bates with his knife. Alicia tried to push away the hypodermic that was heading for her, not in a careful, *let me put a tiny hint of paralyzing toxin in your wrinkles* kind of way, but more like a *let me kill you with a full syringe of deadly poison plunged into your body* way.

Toni could see that Alicia didn't have the strength to fight the woman off for long, but also that Sondra wasn't trying so very hard to kill her. She had the momentary impression of a cat toying with a mouse before finally killing it.

"You should have let him go. He's mine," Sondra screamed, the hand holding the hypodermic waving around.

"Have him," Alicia panted. She was pushed all the way to the edge of the bed. "I don't want him."

"You were so greedy! You had to have all your money. He earned that money living with you. And I definitely earned it. I want it."

This time, when Sondra raised the hypodermic needle, Toni could see that she was going to kill Alicia.

Toni had no weapon with her. All she had was her wits. "Well, you're not going to get her money, or her husband," she said, loud and clear from behind Sondra.

The woman had a gun in one hand and the syringe in the other, but it was clear she didn't want to shoot. She still thought she could pull off her insane plan.

Now, Sondra danced between the two of them, stabbing the syringe toward one and then the other, bobbing lightly like a boxer. Toni had the strangest impression that she was enjoying herself. Enjoying her deadly power.

Toni had noticed a connecting door but thought nothing of it until someone started banging on it. "Who are you talking to? It better not be Lauren or Rose. You are in quarantine." Caitlyn! Bless her tyrannical heart.

"It's TV!" Sondra yelled back. Then, more quietly, "I think I'll kill her when I'm done with you two and do the world a favor."

"Caitlyn," Toni yelled, jumping back. "Call security."

The door opened. "What's going on in there?" And Caitlyn walked through the connecting door, wearing a hospital mask over her mouth. Then took in the scene, her eyes widening. "What the hell?"

"Get out of here," Toni yelled. "Call Security. Call somebody."

She yanked off her mask and yelled. "Ma-a-tt! Get in here."

Not exactly the help Toni had hoped for.

She turned on Sondra. "What are you doing, you crazy bitch?"

"Shut up."

Sondra lunged for Alicia, and as Alicia sidestepped, Toni rushed in from behind and grabbed Sondra around the waist, jerking her around so she faced the other direction.

The woman tried to stab at her hands so she let go and kneed her in the middle of her back, hoping to knock her off balance.

She did knock her off balance. Sondra stumbled toward Caitlyn just as Matt came running in. As Caitlyn tried to back up, she banged into the solid wall of her fiancé, who said, "What the hell?" As Sondra fell forward, the hypodermic plunged into Caitlyn's breast.

The bride screamed, holding her chest as she fell to the ground. Sondra screamed, as she fell, the gun falling to the floor.

"Honey," Matt said, dropping down beside his bride-to-be. "Honey."

Toni grabbed the gun as banging began on the main door. Before she could open it, there was an almighty crash and Alexei burst into the room, gun first. Behind him came Wade and Tiffany.

They all blinked. The bride was on the floor, screaming, Matt beside her looking sick and terrified.

"Quick," Toni said to Sondra, training the gun on her. "There must be an antidote."

A smug, evil smile flashed. "No antidote. She'll be dead within a minute."

Caitlyn screamed again. "Don't listen to her. She's insane. She wrecked my wedding."

Wade ran to his grandmother. "Are you all right?"

She didn't answer, simply clung to him.

Matt was on his knees beside the flailing bride-to-be. Her breasts jerked up and down like two grapefruits under her top. As he reached to pull the hypodermic out of her body, Toni yelled, "Wait. Don't touch that."

"Get it out of me!" the bride shrieked.

"No." Toni strode forward. No natural breasts held that shape when a woman was lying down. "You've got your gel pads in, right?"

"Shut up!"

"Stay still. They may save your life." She turned back to Matt, who wavered, wanting to help the screaming bride, but obviously out of his depth in this whole thing. "Don't touch that syringe."

Tiffany stepped closer and knelt on Caitlyn's other side. "I think Mama's right," she said softly, and her soothing words calmed the crazed bride a little. "So long as the toxin stays sealed inside the gel pad, you should be safe. I know it's completely gross, but I think you should stay very still until a doctor can get here."

Alexei, meanwhile, had Sondra's hands behind her back and was handcuffing her. He was the kind of man who carried plastic restraints in his pocket. A good guy to have around in an emergency.

Pretty soon, the small stateroom was filled with people. The doctor arrived. Over the noise from the still-screaming bride, Toni explained about the gel pads. He had to sedate Caitlyn before she became still enough that they could take her to the medical center. They wheeled her away and Matt followed, wailing, "I'm sorry, baby. I'm so sorry."

The next to arrive was the captain, along with two junior officers. He listened to the story in growing amazement and Toni imagined that in sixteen years, he'd never dealt with anything like this before. "I'm arresting this woman," Alexei said, showing his ID. "You have a brig, I assume?"

"Of course. She'll be confined until we get to port."

"Don't think this is over," Sondra yelled as the three officers took her away. "Because this is not over!"

Alexei looked at Toni. "I thought you killed the doc. Sorry about that."

"It's okay. I thought *you* killed him."

He shook his head.

"Oh," she said, "You might want to look in the bottom right-hand drawer of that desk."

Those hard eyes never changed expression, but he was across the room in two strides. He lifted the medical bag out. Nodded. "Thanks."

Then he left.

Alicia and Wade sat side by side on the bed. "You okay, Grandma?"

"I think I need to go to my room and lie down."

"Sure. I'll take you."

He put an arm around Alicia and helped her to her feet.

As they walked by, he glanced at Toni and Tiffany. "You okay?"

"Yeah," Tiffany said. "Come on, Mom. Let's go shock Grandma." Then she shook her head so her long hair swung. "Again."

CHAPTER 21

Natural beauty takes at least two hours in front of a mirror.

— PAMELA ANDERSON

"Happy birthday, honey," Toni said.

"I think this is the best birthday ever," Tiffany said. "But then, every day your mom isn't killed by a psycho is a good day."

The wedding had, surprisingly, gone ahead as planned. Caitlyn had been incredibly lucky. The needle had lodged in the gel pad and hadn't penetrated through to her skin. After a sedative-induced night's sleep, she'd elected to go through with the wedding.

Amazingly, so had Matt.

Since they were short one bridesmaid, Caitlyn asked Tiffany to step in. Tiff was gorgeous, brunette, and could fit into Sondra's gown. It was the perfect solution.

The makeup was, naturally, flawless. The bride was on her best behavior...or possibly still under the effects of the sedative. It was hard to tell. The captain performed the ceremony. In his uniform. And his British accent added a certain solemnity to the ceremony in the cruise ship's chapel.

Afterward, the party started.

It was their last night at sea and everyone, it seemed, had dressed up and was out on the deck enjoying the warm, balmy night.

Tiffany had changed into a simple white cotton dress and sandals, and wore the silver earrings her mom had given her. "I can't believe I'm seventeen."

Wade walked out on the deck, heartbreakingly handsome in a blazer that had probably been hand-stitched in Italy, with a white shirt and jeans that had probably also been hand-stitched in Italy.

Toni watched him search the deck and saw the way his face lit up when he saw her daughter. He was holding a gift-wrapped box and when Tiffany caught sight of him, she ran forward.

"She's growing up so fast, I can hardly stand it," Toni said to her mom.

Wade raised a hand when Tiffany got close and pushed her hair behind one ear. Their gazes locked.

"I know. And if we keep watching, we're going to witness a grown-up kiss."

They turned away abruptly.

The entertainment directors were out in force, leading the twist and a conga line, and the live band filled the air with music.

Alicia even made an appearance, wearing a white evening gown that showed off her slim figure. She was skilled enough with cosmetics that she'd covered up the parts of her face that were still healing. Toni had to admit that she looked fantastic.

"How are you holding up?" Toni asked.

Alicia breathed deeply of the night air. "I think there are moments in your life when you realize how lucky you are. When Wade came into that stateroom yesterday, and I could see how frantic he was for my safety, I realized what a very lucky woman I am. Also, after yesterday, I'm pretty much over David."

Linda took Alicia to one side and soon they were deep in conversation. Linda pointed to the wrinkles that bothered her and it was pretty easy to figure out what they were talking about.

They only broke apart when Roy walked up to Linda and asked her to dance. Wade danced with Tiffany, and while Toni stood watching, the retired colonel who had helped her when they discovered Dr. Madsen's body asked Alicia to dance. They looked good together, both upright and distinguished. Wealthy or not, Alicia was not going to have trouble finding her next partner. Toni only hoped that her recent experiences had helped her realize how special she was.

While she was watching the dancers, Alexei appeared at her side. "You want to dance?"

"You dance?"

"You'd be surprised at my talents."

Then he led her out to the dance area and impressed her with his jive moves. He started her off slowly but when it was clear she could keep up, he twirled her, spun her, and dipped her. "You can dance," she said, when she could breathe again.

"You're not so bad yourself." He stopped a passing waiter

and ordered them both a drink. "You think you'll ever go on another cruise?"

"Sure. I figure the chances of my ending up on another ship with both a murderer and a heroin smuggler would be like lightning striking twice."

He shook his head. "I don't know, Toni. Something tells me you're the kind of woman that lightning follows around."

She wasn't certain if that was meant as a compliment or not, so, instead of answering him, she sipped her drink.

Toni was contemplating calling it a night when Ryan from Brisbane jumped up on the side of the pool, their makeshift stage, and said into the mic, "Now, ladies and gentlemen, it's time for some line dancing."

Toni glanced up to see Linda extract herself from Roy's arms. She strode across the deck/dance floor and hopped up beside Ryan and took the mic right out of his slack grasp. Linda had chosen a white pantsuit with so much glitter on it that when she held the mic up out of his reach, she looked like the Statue of Liberty. Then she spoke into the microphone. "Honey, you're a sweet young man, but I think it's time you had someone show you how line dancing's supposed to go."

The band had already begun a few bars of a Beatles song when she waved up to the bandleader. "You boys know 'Achy Breaky Heart'?"

The lead singer glanced at Ryan, who shrugged and mouthed, *Why not?* "Sure do, ma'am. You give us a minute."

Linda glanced around until she spotted Toni and then Tiffany. "Ladies?" she called.

"Excuse me," Toni said. And went to join her mother.

Half a minute later, Tiffany jumped up to join them.

As the first bars of "Achy Breaky Heart" began, Linda said, "Y'all can learn a lot from three women from Texas." She grinned at her daughter and granddaughter. "Right, girls?"

"Right, Grandma."

Linda turned back to the crowd now gathered in front of her, including Ryan from Brisbane and the rest of the entertainment crew. She spoke into the mic as she started to move, her daughter and granddaughter following her steps as they'd been doing for years. "And here we go!"

A Note from Nancy

Dear Reader,

Thank you for reading *Midnight Shimmer*. I am so grateful for all the enthusiasm the *Toni Diamond Mysteries* has received.

I hope you'll consider leaving a review and please tell your friends who like cozy mysteries.

Review on Amazon, Goodreads or BookBub.

Don't let the fun end. Let's stay in touch.

Join my newsletter to hear about my new releases and enjoy prizes and bonus content like the Vampire Knitting Club's free prequel, *Tangles and Treasons*, the exciting tale of how the gorgeous Rafe Crosyer was turned into a vampire.

I hope to see you in my private Facebook Group Nancy Warren's Knitwits where the fun continues daily.

Until next time,
Happy Reading,

Nancy

ALSO BY NANCY WARREN

The best way to keep up with new releases, plus enjoy bonus content and prizes is to join Nancy's newsletter at NancyWarrenAuthor.com or join her in her private FaceBook group Nancy Warren's Knitwits.

Toni Diamond Mysteries

Toni Diamond is a successful saleswoman for Lady Bianca Cosmetics in this series of humorous cozy mysteries.

Frosted Shadow - Book 1

Ultimate Concealer - Book 2

Midnight Shimmer - Book 3

A Diamond Choker For Christmas - A Holiday Whodunnit

Toni Diamond Mysteries Boxed Set: Books 1-4

Vampire Knitting Club: Paranormal Cozy Mystery

Lucy Swift inherits an Oxford knitting shop and the late-night knitting club of vampires who live downstairs.

Tangles and Treason - A free ebook for newsletter subscribers. A paperback version is available for sale. NancyWarrenAuthor.com

The Vampire Knitting Club - Book 1

Stitches and Witches - Book 2

Crochet and Cauldrons - Book 3

Stockings and Spells - Book 4

LARGE PRINT EDITIONS: Vampire Knitting Club

Available in paperback or hardback large print format.

Vampire Knitting Club: Cornwall: Paranormal Cozy Mystery

Boston-bred witch Jennifer Cunningham agrees to run a knitting and yarn shop in a fishing village in Cornwall, England—with characters from the Oxford-set *Vampire Knitting Club* series.

The Vampire Knitting Club: Cornwall - Book 1

Scallops and Sorcerers - Book 2

Village Flower Shop: Paranormal Cozy Mystery

In a picture-perfect Cotswold village, flowers, witches, and murder make quite the bouquet for flower shop owner Peony Bellefleur.

Peony Dreadful - Book 1

Karma Camellia - Book 2

Highway to Hellebore - Book 3

Luck of the Iris - Book 4

Game of Thorns - Book 5

Vampire Book Club: Paranormal Women's Fiction Cozy Mystery

Seattle witch Quinn Callahan's midlife crisis is interrupted when she gets sent to Ballydehag, Ireland, to run an unusual bookshop.

Crossing the Lines - Prequel

The Vampire Book Club - Book 1

Chapter and Curse - Book 2

A Spelling Mistake - Book 3

A Poisonous Review - Book 4

In Want of a Knife - Book 5

Vampire Book Club Boxed Set: Books 1-3

Great Witches Baking Show: Paranormal Culinary Cozy Mystery

Poppy Wilkinson, an American with English roots, joins a reality show to win the crown of Britain's Best Baker—and to get inside Broomewode Hall to uncover the secrets of her past.

The Great Witches Baking Show - Book 1

Baker's Coven - Book 2

A Rolling Scone - Book 3

A Bundt Instrument - Book 4

Blood, Sweat and Tiers - Book 5

Crumbs and Misdemeanors - Book 6

A Cream of Passion - Book 7

Cakes and Pains - Book 8

Whisk and Reward - Book 9

Gingerdead House - A Holiday Whodunnit

The Great Witches Baking Show Boxed Set: Books 1-3

The Great Witches Baking Show Boxed Set: Books 4-6 (includes bonus novella)

The Great Witches Baking Show Boxed Set: Books 7-9

Abigail Dixon: 1920s Cozy Historical Mystery

In 1920s Paris everything is très chic, except murder.

Murder at the Paris Fashion House - Book 1

Death at Darrington Manor - Book 2

The Almost Wives Club: Contemporary Romantic Comedy

An enchanted wedding dress is a matchmaker in this series of romantic comedies where five runaway brides find out who the best men really are.

The Almost Wives Club: Kate - Book 1

Secondhand Bride - Book 2

Bridesmaid for Hire - Book 3

The Wedding Flight - Book 4

If the Dress Fits - Book 5

The Almost Wives Club Boxed Set: Books 1-5

Take a Chance: Contemporary Romance

Meet the Chance family, a cobbled together family of eleven kids who are all grown up and finding their ways in life and love.

Chance Encounter - Prequel

Kiss a Girl in the Rain - Book 1

Iris in Bloom - Book 2

Blueprint for a Kiss - Book 3

Every Rose - Book 4

Love to Go - Book 5

The Sheriff's Sweet Surrender - Book 6

The Daisy Game - Book 7

Take a Chance Boxed Set: Prequel and Books 1-3

For a complete list of books, check out Nancy's website at NancyWarrenAuthor.com

ABOUT THE AUTHOR

Nancy Warren is the USA Today Bestselling author of more than 70 novels. She's originally from Vancouver, Canada, though she tends to wander and has lived in England, Italy and California at various times. Favorite moments include being the answer to a crossword puzzle clue in Canada's National Post newspaper, being featured on the front page of the New York Times when her book Speed Dating launched Harlequin's NASCAR series, and being nominated three times for Romance Writers of America's RITA award. She has an MA in Creative Writing from Bath Spa University. She's an avid hiker, loves chocolate and most of all, loves to hear from readers! The best way to stay in touch is to sign up for Nancy's newsletter at www.nancywarren.net.

To learn more about Nancy and her books
www.nancywarren.net